A PIRATE'S BOUNTY

A DEVILS OF THE DEEP NOVELLA

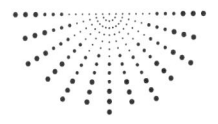

ELIZA KNIGHT

KNIGHT MEDIA

Copyright 2011, 2017 © Eliza Knight

A PIRATE'S BOUNTY © 2011, 2017 Eliza Knight. ALL RIGHTS RESERVED. No part or the whole of this book may be reproduced, distributed, transmitted or utilized (other than for reading by the intended reader) in ANY form (now known or hereafter invented) without prior written permission by the author. The unauthorized reproduction or distribution of this copyrighted work is illegal, and punishable by law.

A PIRATE'S BOUNTY is a work of fiction. The characters and events portrayed in this book are fictional and or are used fictitiously and solely the product of the author's imagination. Any similarity to real persons, living or dead, places, businesses, events or locales is purely coincidental.

Cover Design by Kim Killion @ The Killion Group, Inc.

This book was originally published in 2011 and has been extensively revised for re-release.

A darkly sensual pirate tale of passion and intrigue...

1764 ~ When Faryn is captured by the mysterious and sensual dread pirate Captain Wraith Noir, who delivers her as a slave to the flesh-hungry court of the pirate queen, she expects her future will be bleak and death imminent. Lucky for Faryn, Wraith offers a different destiny—he wants her for his own.

Little does she realize that he's discovered she will help him clear his name. Betrayed many years ago, he sought out the pirate life in an effort to survive and reclaim what was his. But he didn't count on falling for his bounty…

Duty, desire, passion, revenge and treachery besiege Faryn and Wraith. With the future uncertain, only fate, love and the truth will set them both free.

Dear Reader,

This novella was originally published in 2011 as an erotic pirate tale. I have rewritten it, taming it somewhat from its original version, but be warned, the story itself is still quite heated…

Many of the places named within the book do exist, but I have also changed the names of some properties, towns, and names of people for the sake of the story and to fit in with the Pirates of Britannia world.

While this book is a part of the world, it takes place several hundred years in the future from my original two stories.

I do hope you enjoy this dark, pirate tale!

Best wishes,

Eliza

CHAPTER ONE

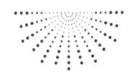

The Coast of the Greek Isles, 1764

The crack of the whip stung as it struck the flesh of Faryn's bare buttocks. She bit hard on the inside of her cheek, refusing to cry out as she knew the crew liked to hear. She would not try to jump overboard again.

Metal clanked against the masts as men shouted, "Heave! Ho!" to get the sails down now that they'd come into port. Instead of a white sail flying prominently against the mainmast, this ship's sail was a flag. Large and intrusive, its image would shake any ship or person who neared it. Eerie wisps of clouds dusted the night sky, and the large silvery moon shone in flashes on the design, which sent an involuntary shudder through her now, just as it always did. Against the wide black backdrop, sewn in white, a large skull, and beneath it two silver swords crisscrossed. Below that was clearly an image in white of the top half of a man, well muscled, who held the two swords.

"School your hands, mate! Orelia will not be pleased that ye marred the flesh of one of her slaves." The voice was filled with authority, and though he spoke English, she noted a slight undertone of a Scot's dialect, something she ought to remember as he could prove to be an ally, but as soon as the thought entered her mind, it was quickly gone again.

Slave.

The word echoed in Faryn's mind over and over in tune to the throb of the welt on her flesh. She looked around with glazed eyes. A rough crew this was. Weapons covered their bodies, some crude, some elegant—and so very out of place, with their rough clothing. Half the men wore plaids draped about their waists, and the others leather breeches. They smiled, some with teeth and some without. They leered at her with one or two eyes, some covered with a patch. Some grabbed at their crotches and waggled what little bits of male flesh hid beneath the layers of grubby clothes. Except for one. The captain. He stood out—dark, mysterious, large and eerily handsome. A cut above the rest.

He was dressed completely in black, from shining leather boots leading to mid-calf, black leather breeches, black linen shirt and cape. Across his waist was a swath of plaid fabric, the ends whipping in the wind. His face was darkly tanned, lips covered by a neatly trimmed dark beard on his chin and a mustache. Hard gray eyes stared out at her from beneath raven brows. His hair was not pulled back but left to hang to his shoulders in sleek black locks, and atop that black head was a black cap, various accouterments attached to it. Beyond beads, feathers and bones, she couldn't make out more of what hung from his cap, nor did she care. She was sure she stood staring directly at the devil.

Slave. Slave. Slave.

This was why they'd taken her in the middle of the night. She cursed her sleeplessness and need to walk on the beach that dreadful evening. They'd ripped her from everything she knew, tied her hands behind her back, tossed her over their shoulders and disappeared into the fog. She would be slave to Orelia. But who was Orelia? She'd never heard the name before now.

"Avast, ye wretches, down ye go, else prepare to feed the fish!" a man shouted, as he hobbled up and down the line of slaves on one foot and a wooden pegleg.

From what Faryn had been able to surmise thus far, Mr. Pegleg was the captain's first mate.

The captain's steely gaze held hers, catching her breath in her throat. She was frightened…yet another feeling had her belly twisting into knots.

Without taking his gaze from hers, he flicked his hand toward her and sliced through the rope tying her arms around the mast. He jerked his head toward the other gangplank. Needing no further instruction, Faryn hurried to line up with the other beaten and naked men and women who would serve as slaves to the mysterious Orelia, eager to have her feet walk on steady ground again. They'd traveled far, she was sure, from her home in Ireland. And as she stepped down the gangplank, splinters sinking into the tender flesh of her feet, she was hit with the knowledge that escape would not come easy.

Ocean stretched far and wide. The sounds of water crashing against the shore, and the scents of salt and ocean surrounded her. Loud voices shouted all around, mixed with the creaking of boards, boot heels clicking on wood and other ship sounds. From the dock came people, she could barely make them out with only the small lanterns they carried. Naked bodies trembled and wobbled down the planks in front of her. She was delirious from hunger and pain. Cold and wet.

Gooseflesh rose along her limbs, her flesh stung as her hair whipped violently against her chest.

She cried out and lost her footing. Arms flung out, she sought hold of anything, her hands catching the slippery back of another slave, who jumped forward at her touch. Her knees dropped to the wood of the gangplank, jarring her with pain and shock.

"Get up!" shouted one of the men wielding a whip. But she could not. She was so weak…too tired. Her vision blurred.

"That one willna make it. Captain, ye want her back? Might be best to toss her to the sharks."

Cruel laughter reached her ears. "Ah, Toothless, ye know I'd love to have another wench in my bed, but I willna be stealing from the Queen. Orelia will have all her slaves, half-dead or not."

So, she was dying, and her last moments of life were to be serving a foreign queen. But mayhap this Orelia would know that she, Faryn, was no ordinary slave but Irish nobility. She didn't belong here. Aye, she would plead her case with Queen Orelia and beg to be sent home.

When she looked up, Faryn noticed that the rest of the slaves had departed the ship and she was alone, still crouched on the cold splintery gangplank. The boards shook beneath her and the thunderous methodical thump of boots on wood sounded behind her.

"Stand, slave, or risk another lash of the whip." The captain's voice was softer than it had been before.

Faryn chanced a glance above her and was taken aback once more by his appearance. So dangerous, and yet he'd showed her a kindness before that he didn't have to.

He moved to hold out his hand, the light glinting off a large and sharp sword as his arm gently nudged it. From his other hip swung a black leather cat-o'-nine-tails.

Faryn shuddered. She didn't want to take his hand.

She wanted to disappear. Her hair cascaded down her back like a cloak, and for a fleeting moment, she wished that the cloak of hair could make her invisible. Foolish thoughts of a desperate and scared woman.

She shook her head and tried to stand, almost making it but collapsing again onto the hard wood.

"Will ye take my help now, lass? Or shall I let ye fall another time?" His voice was soft, not at all in tune with his devilish appearance. Again, he held out his hand.

Squeezing her eyes tight, she reached up and placed her cold, trembling fingers into his warm, rough hand. She expected to be roughly yanked to her feet and shoved or whipped the rest of the way down the gangplank. Surprise registered again as he gently lifted her up to her full height. When his gray eyes widened slightly, darkening with hunger as they traced the outline of her body, she was once again reminded how very nude she was. She crossed her legs, covered her mons with a hand and attempted to cover her breasts with one arm, but he only chuckled at her foolhardiness.

"Dinna ye know, *leannan*, I've seen ye without a stitch on, nigh on a month? We stripped ye bare when first we boarded ye upon my ship." He leaned in close, his white teeth showing between two wide masculine lips, and whispered, "I've touched ye. Weighed and measured ye. Found ye ripe for the picking."

Faryn gasped. "Nat!" A shiver raced along her limbs and her traitorous body reacted to the wicked words whispered to her even as her mind abhorred it. She wanted to remember the feel of this devil man's hands on her, but she could not, and part of her wondered if he was simply messing with her head.

"Oh lovely, dinna worry, your maidenhead is still intact. That is Queen Orelia's to take from ye."

Her mind whirled in confusion. Orelia was a woman. How could she possibly do such as he suggested? Unless she meant to only sell Faryn upon gaining her. She would be sold to the highest bidder, no doubt a nasty, foul-smelling nightmare of a man. Well, she vowed, she'd kill herself first.

Unless… There must be a way to escape this fate. The man exuded a sensuality that gave her an idea, though she wasn't certain she could pull it off in her current condition. However, there was only one way to find out—she had to try.

"Please, Captain… What is your name?" She leaned toward him, letting the tips of her breasts rub seductively against his black linen shirt. She shivered from the sensations—her mind warring with her body—she wanted only to entice him and yet she enticed herself as well. She hurried her proposition before words failed her. "I can assure ye my family can pay ye ten times what ye'll receive from…your queen." That was a lie, of course. She might have been borne of Irish nobles, but they'd been wretchedly poor for far too long.

He did not move, nor did his facial expression change. Had she succeeded only in tempting herself? But then she saw a heated flash of desire in his eyes, before he shuttered it.

"Captain Noir." As he said his name, his fingers danced along her waist, over her ribs and just under her breasts. "But ye needna bribe me with…these." He brushed the undersides of her breasts, sending wicked frissons of heat straight between her legs. "Or your money. I do my duty as I see fit."

Faryn gulped. She was hungry for something beyond her imagination. Wicked. Wanton. Why did this terrifying man, this Captain Noir, make her feel like she wanted to lie down beside him, have him crush her, sink into her?

She shook her head again and looked down toward her bare toes. What was she thinking? To give herself to this scoundrel just to get away from a queen who could possibly help her? Once Orelia knew who she was, she wouldn't sell her. And to think she'd been about to disgrace her family.

Faryn blamed it on a month of near starvation.

Her mother and father would never forgive her. And her betrothed! He would surely search the open seas calling every pirate he found into battle only to die at the end of the blade, all to revenge her honor, which moments ago she had been willing to give away. Tears of frustration stung her eyes.

She stepped back from Noir and whipped around, intending to walk the rest of the way down the gangplank, her head held as high as she could possibly hold it under the circumstances.

His hand, rough with calluses, gripped her arm, stopping her. "What is your name, *leannan*?"

"Faryn. Lady Faryn. My father is a powerful man. Ye shall all be punished severely for stealing me away. And I shall rejoice when the cat-o'-nine-tails rips into your bare arse."

The captain had the audacity to smile. Although it wasn't a curving of the lips filled with humor but of cruelty and distaste. He laughed at her.

"Lady Faryn ye are no longer. Ye will serve the queen. Your family's titles mean nothing here. Curb your tongue of threats, for they will only see ye harmed."

Faryn wrenched her arm from Noir, her resolve restored, and stalked down the rest of the gangplank, acutely aware of the air hitting her behind, her thighs, her breasts, places that had never felt the cool air or spritz of seawater before.

"Be wary, lass, for ye have descended upon the first gate of hell, where no earthly man of morals would dare to cross. Our queen is not a queen by divine right but by right of the blade."

Faryn didn't turn back, nor did she take heed to what he had to say, though she did shudder.

∼

WRAITH WATCHED the sway of creamy white buttocks as the raving beauty walked determinedly away. Despite her being aboard ship for thirty days, her long golden hair still held luster as it hugged her body and waved with the breeze. He imagined running his fingers through her hair, gripping it in his fist and giving it a gentle tug. He couldn't help but smile, for never had he met a woman as tart of tongue and simultaneously innocent as the day she was born.

Cruel world that it was, she would be wasted on the hedonist ways of the queen, then most likely tossed to the wharf.

Dammit, he wanted her!

For himself.

She was a right beautiful woman but beyond her beauty there was something more. Her fiery spirit stirred his blood. And he'd a need to set foot in Ireland. This blonde vixen might be the key to his entry.

The queen did owe him a hefty sum for bringing the nearly two-dozen slaves this trip had proffered. However much he abhorred doing her dirty work of transporting her sex slaves, at least she kept her mouth shut about his true identity. Perhaps he could convince Orelia that instead of his usual charge for shipment, he would take half and the lass. Indeed, she would have only sold Lady Faryn to some sop for less than he would bargain for her.

Och, he had a mind to see it done and have the little filly, Faryn, warming his bed this very night with her gratitude.

CHAPTER TWO

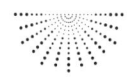

Queen Orelia's castle was warmer than the ship, by far. Even the marble floor was warm to the touch on Faryn's bruised and frozen feet, as if hot rocks had only just been removed from its surface. Yet, Faryn still had the urge to rub her arms furiously to ward off her chill. A chill that she didn't think would go away no matter how warm her environment.

The slaves were lined up in a great hall that was dimly lit with sconces on the stone walls, the wax dripping down the candles along the walls and into creamy puddles on the floor. Faryn gazed around the hall, taking in the elegant columns with vines climbing their way around the marble until reaching the ceiling. Exotic flowers and plants filled the corners and tabletop surfaces. A fountain stood in the middle of the room in the shape of a Greek goddess, looking so much like Dido, a temptress carved in marble, her beauty and sensuality emanating from the stone. Dido's statuesque form poured blood-red liquid from a pitcher into the mouths of a carved nude male and female who knelt before her in supplication. Their bodies were connected in an embrace, heads upturned, mouths open, both receiving what she offered. Wine, not water.

Where was she? What was this place?

She recalled stories regaled to her in her youth of places such as this. Where queens reigned supreme and wantonness was a daily ritual…

As Faryn watched the fountain, mesmerized by its uniqueness and sensuality, several male and female servants, dressed in only silver-chained loincloths, their torsos bare, entered the great hall. She gasped in shock at their near nudeness, even though she herself was completely without clothes. They walked past the fountain, scooping the wine into their own pitchers.

They approached the newly gotten slaves, who stood in a row, Faryn all the way at the end, as she'd been last to enter. The servants passed down the line, pouring wine into the slave's parched mouths. When a female slave approached Faryn, she forgot about wanting to resist anything of this place and opened her mouth, greedily taking in the sweet wine. The female servant continued to pour until wine dripped from Faryn's mouth, over her chin, down her neck and body. Nay, she was thirsty, but not *that* thirsty.

Faryn closed her mouth, wine splashing over her closed lips. She tried to back away but someone held her in place from behind, pulling her arms back so her chest was thrust out and she couldn't move. Her back pressed against warm hard flesh—a male chest. The female servant who stood in front of Faryn leaned forward, her exotic jasmine scent mixing with the aroma of wine, as she gazed into Faryn's eyes, assessing.

The woman pulled a linen square from somewhere and started to wipe away the spilled wine along Faryn's chin and neck. When she moved to Faryn's breasts, Faryn resisted, wanting to clean herself up. With a strength she'd not known she had, Faryn yanked her arm from the man's grasp behind her and ripped the linen from the woman's fingers.

"Dinna touch me," she hissed.

The two of them only laughed and moved on to the next person in line. Another woman. But she did not resist their ministrations. If anything, she relented, closing her eyes. And Faryn was too shocked not to watch as the man and woman licked the wine from the other woman's body.

Fingers roved between the woman's legs, touching her in her most private place. Faryn gaped as the slave moaned at the touch. Gaped wider when her own body sparked a little twinge of something foreign and wicked.

More wine was poured over the woman's body and then more mouths were upon her, sucking up the sweet liquid and tasting her flesh.

Faryn backed away, her legs growing weak. What was happening?

'Twas as if she'd been brought to a brothel. An oddly elegant and majestic brothel.

The lot them appeared delirious with pleasure. Eyes rolling back into their heads as lips, tongues and fingers stroked every part of each other. The other slaves in line, too, looked just as shocked as Faryn. Cheeks flamed red, eyes wide.

Before she could wrap her mind around what was happening, a shriek of pleasure left the slave's lips and her body convulsed. Faryn's own body pulsed with an unbidden hum.

Dear God, what was this place? The first gate of hell, Captain Noir had called it. But why Faryn? What had she done to deserve to be banished to hell? Queen Orelia's den was an erotic nightmare.

She had to get away from here.

And then, from across the grand hall, her eyes locked on Captain Noir himself, a dark expression on his ruggedly handsome face that made her unsteady on her feet.

Mo chreach!

Was Orelia truly choosing so quickly?

Wraith hadn't even a chance to enter the great hall before they were upon Faryn, for devil's sake!

He stood, paralyzed, and somehow able to keep his mouth closed as the two assessors approached her, poured wine on her. Then his pride soared as Faryn took control of the situation, and they moved the next woman in line. But that didn't get the sensual thoughts that were sparked out of Wraith's mind. He imagined Faryn, her body writhing in pleasure, mouth half-open in a silent moan, eyes closed tightly as four of Orelia's servants pleasured her. Mouths on her breasts, mouth on her pearl, hands brushing all over her flesh. Och, watch it would be like to see her climax, legs shaking, a moan of pleasure on her lush lips. The image was so blinding and real, his body reacted violently, cock twitching.

Jealousy filled him at the thought of anyone in this room touching her but him.

She was supposed to be his. He wanted to be the one to give Faryn pleasure.

And there was no time to waste, as he caught sight of Orelia from across the room, her own gaze riveted on Faryn. She twitched her fingers and the two assessors moved back to Faryn. *Ballocks*! Now or never. He stepped forward.

"Step away from the woman, ye heathens."

The servants pulled back, their eyes filled with

uncertainty. Lids lifted and a pair of startling glassy blue eyes locked with his. *Faryn*.

He clenched his teeth and hissed a breath. She was so beautiful, and from the look on her face, completely mystified. Seeing her thus only reaffirmed his goal to have her. Hell, he'd fight off every one in this great hall if he had to.

"Now, now, Captain Noir. Tsk, tsk," came the queen's voice as she melted from the shadows. How many times had he seen her come away from some darkened corner, pleasure filling her eyes at having seen her servants bring a slave, male or female, to fruition? "Would you rob me of my pleasure so soon?"

As if on command, four-dozen, at least, armed guards also stepped from the shadows, prepared to put him in the ground. And he had no doubt, as he'd seen them do just that the last time he was here to another bloke. Wraith was a damned good warrior, but not against nearly fifty men—those just weren't good odds.

Wraith stifled a curse and bowed resentfully low to her. "Queen Orelia, my most humble apologies."

Orelia walked forward, her white gown a cloud of fabric, her jet-black hair floating in waves behind her. If she hadn't named herself queen and been called so he would have thought her royalty anyway…but of a different world. Her eyes were as black as her hair and her lips as red as the blood that he'd seen flow on this very floor. She reached him and a long slender arm emerged from her gown, a red-tipped nail trailed its way up from his navel to his chin.

"I've missed you, Captain." Her voice was breathy, and if it had been a decade earlier, he would have melted into a sodden mess on the floor. Done anything she wanted. But now he'd grown older, wiser. He wanted his life back.

He grasped her hand to stop its traveling over his person and brought it to his lips, kissing her knuckles before letting it drop. "I live to serve ye, Madame."

She snickered and turned her black gaze onto Faryn, whose glassy eyes had come back to their glittering blue sharpness.

"You like her," Orelia remarked, her chin jutting out toward Faryn.

"She has nice breasts," he answered, not wanting to give away totally how he felt about her. "Her thighs are trim, her arse... 'tis lush."

Orelia laughed, her head dipping back, exposing her throat. "You are still the same, Noir. You want her, don't you?"

"I've a mind to bargain with ye."

Her sharp black gaze lost its teasing as she whipped her head toward him. "A bargain?"

"Aye. I thought to speak to ye about it, perhaps later." All eyes had now turned on them. If it was seen how much he wanted Faryn for himself the price would increase, or another man might step forward to fight him for her.

He was prepared to fight for her to the death, for keeping her for himself would not only garner him a warm and luscious bedmate but also secure his future. But revealing such amongst this den of vipers could cost him a far greater price than he wanted to pay. It could also mean the safety of the wench.

"Perhaps now, Captain." Orelia's gaze roved over him, and he could nearly hear her calculating mind at work.

"'Tis of no great consequence, Madame." He shrugged, trying to keep himself looking disinterested even while his pulse quickened. "Do with the slave as ye will for now and I shall speak with ye regarding her fate after I've seen to my men and myself."

Orelia's lips curled. "I should like to see you…do with my new slave."

Wraith raised a brow, hiding his disgust with the queen and her ring of sex slaves. "And by that, ye mean what exactly?"

The queen walked toward Faryn, who now stood tall next to the servants who'd earlier provided her with a taste of pleasure. Orelia trailed her nails along the flesh of Faryn's shoulders, down the valley between her breasts. He watched with barely restrained fury. Faryn's brows drew together, about to rebel, until she caught his subtle shake of his head. If she would only listen, they could both get out of here quickly.

He didn't want her to rebel against him; he wanted her to want him. He pushed the thought aside. Unfortunately, for now, they were both at the mercy of Orelia.

Orelia faced Faryn and lifted her chin. The queen turned Faryn's face from side to side, inspecting her. Her long red fingernails trailed over Faryn's body. Faryn bit her lip. Her eyes met Wraith's and he wanted to step forward and haul Orelia away from his woman.

His woman? She wasn't his and he couldn't think of her that way. She was a possession. And when he took her from here, she would not be his in the sense that first came to mind. Nay, she'd not be *his*. That implied a relationship, and for what she was going to give him, freedom... She would have to be discarded in the end.

"You are so ripe, young slave." Orelia leaned forward, breathing in the scent of Faryn's hair. Faryn only lifted her chin higher. "You know what I think? We have a virgin." Orelia shrieked with triumph and turned around to face Wraith. Her eyes were wide with excitement; however, their depths were not filled with happiness but something more sinister. "You know what this calls for, Captain?"

He raised a brow, knowing very well what it

called for. While Faryn's features remained passive, her gaze told him something else altogether—she stared straight ahead, challenge in her eyes.

Orelia lifted the hem of her white gown and pulled it up her thigh, revealing a small-jeweled dagger. "We must spill the virgin's blood!"

CHAPTER THREE

Faryn tried not to react to the words Orelia spoke or the way the light glinted off the jeweled dagger at her thigh.

Spill her blood? Did they mean to kill her? Was her end to be a virgin sacrifice? A shudder passed through her.

"Orelia, my queen," Captain Noir drawled out. He drew closer to the queen and Faryn watched as the other woman's chest rose more rapidly. Her lids grew heavy. Her reaction showed Faryn that this queen was half-besotted with the captain. Noir traced a finger over the queen's chin. "I am willing to bargain for the lass as she is. Not tattered."

Orelia's lip puckered out in a pout. She stroked her fingers down the length of Noir's chest and lower still to his manhood. She gripped him tightly through his breeches. Faryn watched, mesmerized. When she lifted her gaze, the captain was looking at her, his dark eyes filled with…passion? Aye, passion. Desire.

Did that passion stem from his desire for her or for the woman who held him in her palm?

His lips curved wickedly and he winked at her. Faryn gulped. He was most definitely trying to get a rise out of her.

Dear God in heaven, what was she to do?

She must escape. She glanced around the palace hall but her gaze was pulled back to the captain. He had removed the queen's hand and shoved another pirate in his place. The queen and the newcomer embraced, their mouths meeting in a kiss. A carnal kiss. Their lips slanting over and over. Their tongues danced in and out of each other's mouths. All the while, the captain stared at her. Faryn found herself licking her lips. Wishing she too could share in a kiss like that.

Wicked girl! What was she thinking? To have such thoughts… Her family would be ashamed! Her betrothed would surely break their engagement. This place was bad. Very bad. And yet…

Her eyes were opened to so much surrounding her. Her mind could never forget the experiences she'd had, the things she'd seen and felt.

She flicked her gaze to the floor, where she tried

to count the marks of imperfection in the marble. She'd only gotten to four before a pair of black leather-booted feet came into view.

"*Leannan.*" The captain held out his hand to her.

Take it and she was saying aye to this fate. Run, her mind screamed. Run and never look back!

She took his hand, the flesh and bone overwhelming her own with its sheer size, and she was by no means a dainty miss. Faryn was the height of most men, although slender.

"Ye are mine now, lass." He leaned in close, his lips brushing her ear, causing a shiver to race along her spine. "But even the bargain I struck doesna make ye free from the queen. She has a request."

Faryn looked up into dark eyes, hoping to find a measure of comfort in them. For this was her champion who would take her away from this place, even if it was to be his slave in return. Somewhere, deep inside him, she sensed goodness. Although not readily visible on the surface, she felt it. She trusted her instincts most of the time. Could she trust them now?

"A-a request?" she stammered, unable to get control of her vocal cords.

"Aye, *leannan.*"

Faryn peered over his shoulder and watched as the servants ushered the other slaves from the room. Orelia slinked into the background, seemingly melding into the shadows from which she'd emerged.

"Captain, we both know that I am a well-educated woman—unless, that is, ye are not aware that a woman of my status would have been taught a few things, unlike a common serving wench. Tell me no lies, Noir, for I am not naïve as ye may have convinced yourself."

The captain took her by the elbow and guided her into a dimly lit corner.

"It is not often we have a virgin come to Orelia's court, *leannan*. Ye heard her speak of spilling virgin's blood?"

"Aye, she means to sacrifice me to whatever gods it is she prays to." Or preys upon. Faryn lifted her gaze to the ceilings, for the first time noticing their domed design with intricate scene paintings, but the tears pooling in her eyes blinded her vision.

"Dinna speak ill of her, for she is willing to be kind to ye. Instead of sacrificing ye, she is allowing for another type of blood."

Faryn frowned, her gaze returning to the captain's. "Well?" she said in mock exasperation, hoping he did not see through her bravado.

"She will allow for virgin's blood to be spilled… In other words, your maidenhead to be taken in front of witnesses."

Faryn felt every single drop of blood rush from her face down her neck and into her chest, before pooling in her stomach like burning lava. She was going to retch.

"Lass," the captain said, but his voice sounded hollow, distant. "Dinna be so discontent. For the price of your virginity, she is willing to let ye go with me. And I am willing to rethink your earlier bargain."

Faryn glanced around her, her eyes glassy. The captain's lips continued to move but she couldn't hear the words that were coming from his mouth.

He gripped her shoulders, appearing to attempt to regain her attention, but she was lost.

Her eyes rolled into the back of her head and she started to fall.

Wraith caught her just in time.

Despite being pale as a ghost, her flesh was warm, the heat of it seeping through his garments.

He wasn't such a monster. He offered her freedom in exchange for one thing. Well, two, he supposed. Virginity and a large sum of her family's fortune. But the payment was nothing compared to the gift he was giving her. Besides, was that not unlike a marriage? The bride often brought her virginity and a dowry to the union. This was the same thing.

Didn't she realize he would take her maidenhead with kindness, give her pleasure in return for her sacrifice?

Ballocks!

The fact that he wanted to give her pleasure at all sent the blood rushing from his face. But he liked to pleasure all women. Why would it be any different with the slave lass?

Her silky hair fell over his arm and she moaned in her unconsciousness.

"You have such a way with the ladies." Orelia laughed as she walked across the room, her gaze roving over the lass in his arms.

Wraith chuckled mercilessly. "Wouldna ye know?"

"I'd like to know again. Now."

"And I want to show ye." His mind revolted at anything having to do with Orelia but in order to gain the girl, he would have to acquiesce to her. "Let me take her to my rooms, where she can sleep away her shock. I shall come to ye directly."

"Nay," Orelia snapped. "That will not do at all."

His gut clenched. What was the ungrateful bitch up to now?

"I await your commands, my queen."

"Tie her to the bed in the sacrificial room." Her lips curled in an angry way, making her beauty diminish a fraction. "You can make love to me lying next to her."

"As ye wish, my queen." How the bloody hell was he going to get out of this? And her calling it making love when it was anything but? Now he was to be the sacrificial lamb.

"Come, my pirate captain, I ache with wanting."

Wraith dutifully followed Orelia, glad of only one thing. If the lovely Faryn lay next to them, at least he would be able to gaze on her and pretend it was she he was lying with and not Orelia. He furiously counted down the days he had left to serve this vicious pirate queen. The day he would owe her nothing.

Nevertheless do his duty now he would, and he would do it well, for it was the only way to escape this place both alive and with his own bargain for freedom. The lass had no idea how much was riding on her. Not only her own life, but also his.

Faryn awoke to the throaty moans and shouts of a woman laying so close it could almost be right in her ear.

Her world was also rocking. Back and forth. Had she been returned to the ship? She tried to sit up but her hands were bound tight to something. She tried to move her feet but they too were bound.

Her world was still black. But then again, she hadn't opened her eyes yet. She blinked.

The moans grew louder, the rocking fiercer. There were sounds of flesh upon flesh. Carnal sounds.

Faryn turned slowly to her right.

Dear Lord! The woman *was* right next to her ear.

Queen Orelia lay next to her. Her eyes were closed in ecstasy as a man, bare, bronzed and full of sinew and muscle, buried his face against her breasts and his fingers digging into her hips as he thrust between her legs…

Faryn gasped, her eyes widened. She looked about her. The room was dark except for the lighted candles surrounding the massive bed. She was bound with white ties about her ankles and wrists. Thank God, they had not gagged her as well.

She opened her mouth to speak, to shout out, but she couldn't find her voice. And even if she did, the sounds the woman was making would surely drown out any pleas she could issue.

Where was the captain? Hadn't he promised her freedom? Safety? Had he lied?

She pulled at the ties but that only seemed to make them tighter.

She glanced around frantically. Trying to see something, anything—what she wasn't sure of. She did know that once she saw whatever it was she was looking for, she would know.

The woman shrieked one last time, her body quivering for what seemed like minute upon minute upon minute, and then she stopped and the man leaning over her stopped thrusting.

"Oh captain, my captain, you still know how to pleasure a woman," the queen crooned.

Captain? Had she truly said captain? Was it Noir who'd pleasured the queen? Faryn's eyes widened as her gaze roved over the man whose face was turned away. The dark hair matched his but truly that was all she could recognize, for she'd only ever seen him clothed, and this man…was most definitely not clothed.

But then she saw him, standing across the room. Captain Noir. He was not the one who'd been with the queen after all. His low voice rumbled as he spoke. The black cape and linen shirt he wore had been removed, and his back was to her.

His shoulders and arms rippled with muscle. His back bulged and flexed as he moved, and the way he stood, she imagined as no lady should, that beneath the tight breeches the most beautiful, muscular, round, hard halves of a male's buttocks were waiting to be discovered. He could have been forged from one of the many godly statues and paintings she'd gazed on. His legs were long, lithe, and strong.

She swallowed hard, belly quivering.

Captain Noir was more than a man. And that was only her impression from seeing him from behind. If he were to turn around… If he were to stand before her and she could see his chest…

Her heart pounded. Her breaths were shallow. Her mouth was suddenly dry. She wouldn't mind at all if Noir, this god were to do the same to her that the other captain had done to the queen.

Was there room to hope? If the queen were insistent that Faryn's virgin's blood be taken… Could it be…? Could he be the one to see to the ghastly farce of bedding her before one and all?

She shook her head, as if doing such a thing would force her thoughts to flit away. There was no hope in this place. Only hedonistic torment it would seem. Besides, she couldn't think of enjoying his body, not when he'd be taking what belonged to her betrothed. Not when she was a lady who shouldn't want him. When she shouldn't desire the pleasure that tingled just beneath the surface of her conscience.

'Twas this place. It was getting into her head.

Aye, she couldn't think of garnering pleasure from this pirate. Nay! She should be outraged. Yet, she was not. If anything, her blood heated. The place between her legs thrummed with need. Ignoring all of her logical thoughts.

Indeed, she would secretly enjoy it if the captain were to climb atop her and thrust himself between her thighs.

She whimpered before realizing the noise had escaped her.

Noir turned from his companions then and, dark stormy eyes locked with hers. His gaze moved over her face, pausing at the lip she had tucked between her teeth down to her rapidly rising and falling chest. Her nipples tingled, already hard and begging for his mouth to clasp the flesh between his teeth, to lick and suckle her.

Her emotions must have flitted across her face, as the captain smiled at her in a devilish and inviting way. He slowly stalked toward her, standing at the foot of the bed. The front of him was even more impressive than his back.

His chest and stomach were sculpted into ridges and valleys tapering down to his navel, where the sprinkling of his chest hair came to a line that led directly beneath his breeches.

"Welcome back, lass," he said smoothly.

Faryn nodded, tugging at the ties.

Her body might have pulsed a tune of anxious anticipation but her mind screamed nay. She couldn't allow this to happen. She had to stall for time. Time for her to figure out a way to escape. She tore her gaze from Noir's magnificent body and stared at the impossibly high ceiling.

Tears pooled in her eyes again. She'd only been in Orelia's lair for a few hours and already she was changing. Already her morals were leaving her. Everything she valued tossed to the wind. Everything she believed in—gone.

The mattress moved beneath her and from her peripheral vision she watched the queen stand and saunter toward the captain.

"You have one hour to prepare her for what is to happen. I will be most disappointed if she doesn't open her legs for you willingly and equally disappointed if she doesn't enjoy it."

Faryn closed her eyes, though she couldn't close her ears.

God help her, she would be ruined.

Yet, she didn't have much choice. Be ruined, or forever a slave in this place.

Faryn chose ruined and free.

CHAPTER FOUR

Desire had filled the innocent depths of the Faryn's eyes as she'd greedily taken in the sight of Wraith's half-nude body. Just as quickly fear, anger and hurt had replaced it and she'd turned away.

He'd seen the calculation in Orelia's eyes as she'd watched the interplay between them. She'd seen a way out of her bargain. A way to keep the girl, who he was sure she wanted for herself.

One hour.

Was one hour enough for him to convince the lass to be willing, to make her pleasure known? Noir was not at all in doubt he could give her pleasure, but asking a shy virgin to show it in front of others was a whole other difficulty.

He pulled on his shirt, hoping that by covering his naked chest he would be able to quell some of her fears, have her listen to and concentrate on his words.

She still stared up at the ceiling and now he could see moisture on her cheeks. She was crying. Pulling a thin sheet from a chest against the wall, he walked slowly forward and sat down on the bed beside her. Gently, he covered her with the sheet, and relief flooded him when she turned her gaze toward his, the hate gone from her eyes.

"Thank ye, but why did ye do that?" Her voice was small, and he hated that.

He hated that she was scared. That this woman who'd come at him with a flashing tongue could be cut down to something so small. Hated that when they'd raided Ireland, she'd been rounded up and tossed below decks. Hated that he'd not even bothered to see who had been taken, and only come to see her when she was being whipped at the mast nearly a month later. He wasn't idiot enough to flatter himself that he would have rescued her for something better had he gone below to the slave hold to see their newly acquired flesh, but he liked to think he might have.

"Ye looked cold," he murmured with a smile.

"Ye lie, Captain." Her words were filled with mirth and accompanied by a small smile. "Ye seek to comfort me. But ye needna do such a thing. I know what I must do, and I promise I will do it. Ye shall have me, ye shall have my family's coin. And I shall be free."

More than her fear, he hated the fact that he would bed her only because she wanted freedom. He wanted her to desire him. He wanted her to beg him. But with a woman of her stature, her moral code, such a thing would be impossible without marriage. Marriage was not up for bargain.

But perhaps he could hint… and that would help to assuage her.

"*Leannan*," he sighed. "I know ye to be of noble birth. And while a pirate may not be who ye'd thought would take away your most valued possession, it is so. If it pleases ye—"

She rolled her eyes and chuckled, shocking him into silence.

"Captain Noir, please dinna tell me ye are about to humble yourself and offer marriage to me?"

He couldn't speak, only stared.

"Ye can if ye wish, but know that I will deny ye. I am betrothed already and he is sure to find us upon the open sea for my wedding date is set to be very soon, and rain holy hell down upon ye."

"Do ye love this man?"

She crinkled up her face and snorted. "Does any woman ever love the man her parents have chosen for her to marry because it will strengthen both families' place in the realm and their coffers?"

"Nay," he said flatly, his lips thinning.

"I sense from your response that perhaps ye were at one time betrothed?" She shifted on the bed, the sheet sneaking down to expose the tops of her breasts.

Why did that bit of flesh entice him more than seeing her nude had? He could imagine every inch of her breasts. Imagine pulling the sheet away with his teeth to nip at her tender flesh.

He snapped his gaze back to hers. "I was once. But 'twas long ago and in another lifetime."

"Truly?" Her eyes narrowed as she tried to read him.

The little imp. "On my honor."

At that, she laughed aloud. "Captain, ye have no honor. Ye're a pirate set to steal ladies from their beds and plunder their riches."

At her choice of words, he too chuckled. He didn't know why but a piece of the steel he'd surrounded himself with to protect his identity opened. This woman was able to wrench a hole in his armor. "'Tis true of me now but I havena always been Captain Wraith Noir, lass. Everyone has secrets."

"Tell me yours."

Her gentle demand was alluring. Made him want to open up to her, to tell her his secrets, confidences that had never passed his lips. *Get hold of yourself, man*! He was about to spill his entire life story in her lap when he should be enticing her to enjoy what they were soon to experience so they could both escape alive.

"If I told ye, they wouldna be secrets anymore."

"So mysterious ye are, Noir. Ye know nearly everything about me, and yet I know nothing about ye."

"'Tis not about the knowing. Besides, I know naught of ye."

She grunted skeptically. "Then what is it about?"

She had him there. How to answer her? Wraith sighed deeply. He was no good at this wooing thing. The women he cavorted with came to him, hopped on his lap and demanded a ride.

He grinned at her and winked. "'Tis about..." He found her fingers and entwined them with his. "This. The sharing. The sealing of one's fate. 'Tis about opening up the most private part of yourself and allowing another to explore it. 'Tis about my soul touching yours in that one moment when earth shatters and disappears, and we travel up into the stars, melding as one being. That moment when nothing else matters but the person in your arms."

"Ye make it sound so... Wonderful."

"It can be."

She swallowed, her throat bobbing as she did so, and the weariness in her eyes had not yet fully melted away.

"I promise, lass, that when we finish, I will take

ye away from here. And I willna touch ye again, unless ye ask me to."

At that promise, there was a tiny melting in her gaze. "How do I know ye mean what ye say?"

"I ask ye to trust me, but I know ye have no reason to."

"Aye."

Wraith brought her hand to his lips and kissed her knuckles gently. "I'm sorry for taking ye away from your home."

"Why?"

God's bones, this was difficult. There were a number of reasons why, but most of them didn't make sense even to him, so how was he supposed to make sense of them to her?

"Because, for one thing, we wouldna be in this situation." He smiled wryly. "But for another, I admit a touch of worry over your betrothed and the supposed holy hell I am to be subjected to."

"Ah, aye, ye will be sorry for it."

"My men are not supposed to take ladies."

"Someone made a mistake then?"

"Aye. And I will see them punished for it."

"Ye would do that? For me?"

"Aye."

"Might I impart some advice, Captain Noir?"

"Ye can try."

She wrinkled her nose. "If your men knew ye were so willing to punish them over me, a mere slip of a lass, they might not respect ye as much as a pirate of your station deserves."

"A pirate of my station? Have ye heard of me afore now?"

She smiled brilliantly, and for a moment, it might have been that they were not here on this bed, but in another place. "Nay," she laughed. "But I do know pirates are supposed to be ruthless."

Wraith ran his knuckles gently up her arm. "I am only ruthless when it comes to battle, lass, and generous when it comes to the lassies."

He wasn't sure which part of what he said exactly made her smile, made the fear slowly ebb, but he was exceedingly happy to see.

"What would ye consider generous?" There was a twinkle in her eye. "Swaths of gold silk, or sharing your best champagne?"

Wraith grinned at her choice of pleasures. "Both, lass, and a satisfied smile to go with them."

"What would make a lass smile like that?" A spark in her eye showed she had an idea, even if only introduced in the last few hours to it.

He wasn't certain, what had changed, but knew she was nearly ready. Her muscles had relaxed, her eyes widened, curiously.

"Do ye want me to show ye? Before they return?"

"Aye," she whispered. Her lips glistened where she licked them.

Wraith could stand it no longer. He didn't care if

one hour had been reached or not. He was going to kiss her. He was going to make her want him and he was doing it now. To hell with the queen. The way to make this performance a success was to go at their own pace, to make Faryn comfortable, and he knew that would be anything but the case if they were surrounded by everyone.

Besides, he had a feeling that Orelia would like very much to walk in on their lovemaking, to be a voyeur.

He leaned forward, one arm bracing beside Faryn to hold him up, and brushed his lips over hers, feeling the warmth of her breath on his mouth as she sighed. She leaned her head up into him, not fighting his kiss at all, and he pressed his lips more firmly on hers. He stayed like that for a moment, breathing in her womanly essence, reveling in the sensation of such a sweet kiss. Taking a deep male satisfaction in that this was probably her first.

He nibbled her lower lip. Licked the crease between her lips. Slanted his mouth over hers, nuzzling and encouraging her to kiss him back. Her lips parted and her soft, warm tongue shyly came out to touch his. He let her explore his lips with her tongue as he had before touching his own tongue to hers.

She gasped when their tongues collided, and shuddered beneath him. Or was it he who shuddered? Perhaps they both had.

He moved to lay atop her, settling his hips between her spread legs, his bare belly to her sheet-clad stomach and his chest pressed against her breasts. The warmth of her seeped through the thin cloth and his shirt, igniting against his flesh, making him burn to tear the thin sheet from her body and feel the delicacy that would be skin on skin. She rubbed her breasts against him, tugged at her restraints. Should he untie her? He wanted to feel her legs wrapped around his hips. He wanted to feel her hands stroke over his back, run through his hair. Aye, he would untie her. And he wouldn't have to worry about her escape, for she knew what was at stake, and her freedom was important but even more so…the sexy little mewls she was making showed that she too was enjoying his kisses and wouldn't be so quick to up and run from his touch.

Perhaps for now he would only untie her arms…

Wraith continued to kiss Faryn, deeply, carnally, his tongue sinking into the depths of her mouth. Giving her what he'd promised, metaphorical golden silk and champagne. She eagerly returned his kiss, startling him for a moment. She was a natural kisser. No virgin's kiss was this. Once again, she'd pleasantly surprised him with her inner fire, her spirit. She would be a passionate lover.

He slid his hands up her arms until he reached the knots that restrained her. Keeping his lips on hers, he untied the bonds that held her, tossing the silky ribbons to the floor.

Immediately her arms came around him, rubbing over his shoulders, exploring the expanse of his back. He let her touch him, get used to the feel of his body while he trailed kisses from her lips to her neck, nipping at the lobe of her ear.

Her head tilted back, eyes closed, Faryn was completely unaware when the air around them grew charged with wanton energy. Orelia had returned and with her the nearly one hundred slaves and servants of the hedonistic castle. They stood 'round the bed and beyond, watching, some pushing for greater view, greed and desire in their eyes. Wraith gave them only a moment's notice before returning to the task of deflowering sweet Faryn.

Tenderly he stroked over her ribs, tugging the sheet down and over her breasts. She clutched his shoulders with both hands. He trailed his tongue from the nape of her neck down her chest to the valley between her breasts. He cupped a breast in each hand, massaging the pink tips with the pads of his thumbs.

"Oh," she murmured, pushing her chest further into him, her breasts filling his hands.

"Aye, Faryn, tell me ye like it."

"Aye…"

"Aye, what?" he teased, his tongue snaking out to flick over a turgid nipple.

She sucked in her breath and crooned her pleasure.

Wraith flicked her nipple again with his tongue and then flicked the other, back and forth, massaging her breasts with his hands until she panted with pleasure.

"Please," she begged.

He knew what she wanted, but did she know? "Please what?"

She bit her lip and opened her eyes a fraction, the once-clear depths now cloudy with desire. He'd never wanted a woman more than he did now. And he didn't think he'd ever seen a woman show so much desire and truth in lovemaking before. All his worries about whether or not she'd be able to pull of this little ruse evaporated. She was a good actress, and she must have realized that the crowd had pushed in.

"Tell me, sweetness, what do ye want?"

"I want…I want ye to…"

"Suck on your nipples?" he murmured, sucking one into his mouth.

"Oh…" Her back arched.

He chuckled against her flesh, delighted in her innocent reaction, her pure expression of pleasure and desire.

She raked her nails down his back, thrusting her chest upward. He answered her call for more, teasing her relentlessly with his mouth against her flesh.

He moved upward and buried his face against her neck, caressing her thighs up and down with his fingertips, tugging the sheet higher and higher.

His pants grew tighter and tighter as his cock engorged. He'd never been harder in his life. What was it about this lass that gave him this reaction?

He couldn't wait any longer to touch the center of her. Shifting to the side, he trailed a hand over her hip, across her flat belly and to the triangle of soft curls covering her core. He moved his mouth to her lips and kissed her gently, teasing her lips as he teased the folds of her sex with his fingers. He found her pleasure bud and stroked over it with his thumb. Faryn moaned into his mouth, her hips bucking upward. He smiled against her mouth, continuing to stroke her pearl as he moved two fingers to slide inside her wet warmth.

She was tight, so damn tight, against his fingers. His cock jumped as he imagined burying himself to the hilt within her. But before he did that, he needed to show her the pleasure he'd promised. He wanted to feel her flutter and clench against his fingers, feel her writhe and pulse beneath him, hear her cries of pleasure before he took her. He wanted to hear her tell him that she wanted him. That she needed him.

Needed. Where had that come from? He'd never wanted anyone to need him before. No indeed. Even scarier was that it wasn't just a *want* for her to need him, he *need*ed her to need him. Wraith thrust the disturbing thoughts aside and focused on the woman beneath him. Her hips moved against his hand as he stroked. Her moans were more frequent, her breathing erratic. The walls of her slick sex grew tighter and tighter as she clenched her muscles.

Then, there it was. The flutter and clench against his fingers that he sought. She writhed beneath him. Fingernails raked down his back, her mouth open against his as she shrieked her pleasure.

Wraith did not wait for her to recover. Instead, he demanded she look at him. Her eyes opened slowly and something jerked inside his chest. Her gaze was passion filled, needy.

"Noir… I…"

"Shh… Just tell me ye want me," he whispered.

"Aye, aye, I want ye," she said quickly.

He unlaced his breeches, too desperate to be inside her to yank them off all the way, only releasing his engorged arousal.

"My legs," she protested. "I want to wrap them around ye."

His blood surged at her words, and he was eager to have her long, soft legs wrapped around him. He'd forgotten all about her legs being tied up. Forgotten all about their audience as well. Someone stepped forward and freed her legs, which she lifted her legs tentatively and curled around his hips. There was a spark of panic in her eyes that made him wonder if she hadn't been aware of their audience after all. He leaned down, their gazes still locked. "Look at me, Faryn. Only me."

She swallowed, her lower lip trembling but still she nodded, eyes fastened on his. Wraith pressed his forehead to hers, kissed her lips, sucking the bottom one into his mouth to still her trembling.

"Will ye say it again, lass?" he murmured.

"Say what?" Her fingers on his shoulders trembled.

"What ye said before," he urged, not wanting to put the words in her mouth, needing her to realize that she had desired him of her own accord.

"I want ye?" she questioned.

"Aye, that."

"I want ye."

"Och, but ye dinna know what that does to me, lass. Tell me ye need me. Ye want me inside ye." He licked at her mouth, pressed his hips against hers, his shaft teasing her folds. Her eyes started to roll back and she let out a soft moan, rocking her hips with him.

"Aye, I need ye. I want ye inside me."

Finally, the moment came where he placed the tip of his arousal at her entrance. Wet, slick, hot… He gritted his teeth in ecstasy as he slowly inched forward until he reached her barrier. His forehead pressed to hers—he wanted to thrust deep inside but had to go slow. He pressed forward. She was tight. Heaven help him... He'd never experienced the pleasure of loving a woman as he did now with this blonde-haired beauty. He wrapped her hair around his fist and tugged lightly. She nipped at the skin of his shoulder and he buried his head further against her neck, sucking at the skin pulsing with her heartbeat.

He sank a little deeper. He'd bedded a virgin once—so long ago he'd nearly forgotten, and now wasn't the moment he wanted to remember, but he'd yet to feel Faryn's maidenhead—and he should have already. Perhaps he remembered wrong and her maidenhead was in a little farther. Soon...he'd be there soon, and then he'd have to drive home, quick and easy as to lessen the pain of it. Inch by inch, painstakingly slow, he plunged a little deeper.

The walls of her center pulsed around him, stretching, and she moaned against his ear. He wouldn't be able to stand the torture much longer.

Faryn arched her back, tilted her hips up and thrust against him, impaling herself all the way. There was no breach, there was no cry of pain.

What the—?

One thing was for damn sure, Faryn was no virgin.

CHAPTER FIVE

Wraith's eyes popped open and he tried to meet Faryn's gaze but her eyes were closed tight against flushed cheeks.

"Are ye all right?" he asked, just in case he had in fact torn through her barrier and not been aware of it.

"Aye." She blinked her eyes open, hazy with desire and wonder. "Please, dinna stop."

Staring into her eyes, Wraith pulled out slowly, then just as slowly eased back in. Faryn moaned, her head falling to the side, legs clenching tight around his hips, and her hands roved over his back.

As much as he wanted to stop, to question her further, he couldn't. His desire for the lass was overpowering. Beneath him, she lifted her hips encouragingly. It felt too damn good. To hell with questioning. He plunged deep inside her, withdrew and drove home again. He gripped her hips, tilting them farther upward as he plundered deeper inside her treasure.

He shouted out encouraging words, her answering cries leading him to a point of no return. His control was lost. On the outskirts of his consciousness he could hear those around them moaning with delight, cheering on the pirate as he took what was his. But that mattered not to him. What mattered was this woman in his arms—that she was a perfect bedmate for him. A match to his lusty desires.

He would enjoy taking her back to her family. There would be many nights upon his ship for him to do this again and again.

Faryn tightened up around him, her back arching as once again she found climax. With four final thrusts, Wraith grunted deep inside her.

They stilled on the bed, both of their breathing labored as they came down from the heavenly height of pleasure.

Bones of the sea devil, what had just happened? Wraith buried his face in the crook of her neck and worked to gather his breath. Never before had he lost control with a woman as he had just now.

∽

FARYN JERKED HER HEAD UP, eyes wide as she stared

at their surroundings. The blood drained from her face and she bit her lip hard to keep from crying out in surprise.

How could she have forgotten where they were?

Her legs were still wrapped around Noir's hips. Her arms still on his shoulders. He was still inside her, although softer now.

How could she have forgotten what was expected? They wanted to see blood on the white sheets.

Orelia stepped forward, a cruel smile on her lips. She clapped her hands slowly.

"My, my, slave. You are an ardent and passionate lover for one who claims to be a virgin." Her cold dark eyes bore into Faryn's gaze before slowly moving to meet Noir's.

Oh, nay! How could she have let herself go so completely? How could she have lost all control and acted the wanton? She knew exactly how. Noir was a masterful lover. His mouth, fingers, body had stirred something primal within her. She'd instinctively heeded the call. But only to her detriment. The queen knew. Faryn felt naïve for thinking she could keep the knowledge of her not being a virgin from their minds. But her loss of virginity was too painful to recollect. Her virtue had been lured from her by lust and empty promises. Had Noir suspected she was not pure? Did he know?

Noir fiddled with something between them. He

turned his gazed toward her own and his eyes flashed warning. Before she could understand the meaning in his expression, a sharp sting came from high up on her thigh, near her groin. She cringed and bit the inside of her cheek to keep from crying out.

His actions answered her question. Once he'd entered her fully he'd been aware she was no virgin and yet still, he'd continued to make love to her. He'd delved inside her body with an exuberance and delight she'd never known possible and he'd pleasured her. He'd cried out to her, whispered nonsensical words of her beauty, of her passion and his desire for her.

Yet, he'd known.

Faryn swallowed hard. She couldn't read too much into it. He was doing what he needed to survive the queen's wrath and to keep Faryn alive. He knew the only way to get her out of here was for her to bleed, and if he didn't get her out of this place, he wouldn't get his coin from her family.

Noir withdrew from her slowly and, using the sheet that had covered her to keep her warm before, he wiped at the inside of her thighs. The sheet came back stained red with blood.

She studied his nails, which were neatly trimmed. How had he cut her?

"The answer to your question could go one of two ways. Either I'm a lucky pirate or I'm that good, my queen." He laughed and showed everyone the stained linen.

Orelia was naturally shocked, as Faryn was sure she'd figured out her secret. Her eyes widened and she nodded. A hungry look came into the queen's eyes. "I see," she said toward Faryn and then turned back to Noir. "You're that good."

Captain Noir stood, putting his breeches and the rest of his clothing back to rights.

Faryn felt suddenly vulnerable. She was on display for all to see. She crossed her legs and her arms over her chest to hide her areas. She turned to Noir, wondering if he would take her to safety now or if his tenderness had been a ruse to get her to willingly spread her legs.

Something glinted on his finger in the candlelight as he handed her the sheet to recover herself. A skull-shaped ring. But it was a strange ring. She narrowed her eyes to look closer and saw that it had a very tiny dagger coming out the length of his finger from the ring. Before she could look further, he pressed a button and the dagger disappeared. So, that was how he'd cut her.

Though it had been a risk to slice her so close to her nether regions, she was grateful for his quick thinking. She'd never seen a weapon like that before, and it sent a shiver running through her. How many others' blood was on that tiny dagger?

"Anyone else want to taste the blood of a virgin?"

Orelia shouted to the crowd, her arms spread wide before she pointed at Faryn.

Faryn started to protest but the captain stepped forward, cutting her off.

"We had a deal, Orelia."

"Deals can be broken." The queen's eyes narrowed.

"Not this time." Noir had a deadly look on his face. Judging from the muscle jerking in the side of his jaw, Faryn would venture to guess he was reaching the limit of his patience. "I'll take my booty and be on my way."

Orelia turned fully toward him, her face away from Faryn. They stood that way in silence for several moments. Neither moved. It was a battle of wills that Faryn was glad she didn't have to participate in.

"You'd best be on your way then, Captain, before I change my mind."

Noir nodded, gripped Faryn's hand and yanked her to her feet.

Orelia's head fell back and she laughed aloud as Noir walked fast, pulling her behind him out through the crowd of undulating, moaning bodies.

"Avast, men! Ye landlubbers! Back to the ship! We sail within the hour or I shall see ye to Davy Jones!" the captain shouted.

At his authoritative words and commanding voice, men pooled around them. The whines of women and men accompanied the loss of their sexual partners as the pirates gathered to serve their master. A servant rushed forward and handed Noir a jingling bag, which Faryn assumed must be his payment for delivering Orelia's shipment.

Faryn stumbled between Noir and his men out of Orelia's lair, to the docks and back up the gangplank. The captain didn't stop, even when she nearly fell to her knees. His strides were determined. He barked orders left and right and all around her, what at first appeared to be chaos was actually quite orderly as the men pulled up anchor, set the sails and prepared to shove off.

Noir took her up a series of narrow short stairways, dodging ship's equipment and men until they entered a large oak door, which he promptly shut behind them. The room was vast with a gigantic bed piled high with pillows and what appeared to be thick blankets made of woven plaid. A large table with several chairs around it stood in a corner, piled high with papers.

Before she had a chance to look anywhere else, her attention was caught by the captain who'd flung open the doors of his wardrobe and was rifling through its contents.

"*Ballocks.*" He came back and rubbed at his chin, still staring into the wardrobe. "Thought I might have had something for ye to put on, a gown or some such, but it appears that whatever women's wear I may have once had on this ship has disappeared."

He grabbed a white linen shirt and tossed it to her.

"Wear that for now. It will at least keep ye somewhat warm." He narrowed his eyes and licked his lips. His gaze fell to where the sheet was pulled taut to her breasts, causing her heart to pump faster. Her belly warmed and a frisson of the same desire she'd felt before flashed through her veins. "Aye, put my shirt on quickly, else I have a mind to take ye to bed again, which at the moment would not be a good idea."

She nodded and tugged his shirt on.

"I'll be back later. The sooner we leave port the better. Orelia is known for changing her mind often."

He left the cabin without a backward glance. She scowled at nothing in particular with the realization that she'd wanted him to embrace her, kiss her before he left. Their lovemaking hadn't felt like a duty but something more. She had to stop thinking on it for it would only bring her disappointment.

Noir was a pirate. He wanted something that she'd promised. That was it. Nothing more. Nothing less.

Faryn sighed heavily. Relief flooded her. They were away from the queen. They were away from the den of vileness. She would be home soon. Relief was replaced with trepidation and then relief again.

Back and forth. What would she do when she returned home? Would she even be accepted? Would her family pay the pirate? Or toss her out?

Knowing her virtue was compromised, there was no telling that her family would want her back. Already she'd been the cause of pain and shame.

A shiver chased down her spine.

Noir would surely punish her if they didn't.

She would have to strike a deal of her own with him. Something he couldn't refuse. But what? Already she'd promised him a fortune from her family. He'd already had her in bed. What more could he want?

She shook her head and sat down on the pirate's large bed.

Hope filled her when she'd realized that she was soon to be going home. But now there was no trace of hope left. Only dread.

~

"Where to, Cap'n?" asked Churl, Wraith's first mate.

"Go west through the Mediterranean Sea. All the way to Ireland. We'll dock at Clew Bay and go to her family's estate by horse. The lass goes home."

Churl raised his brow at that then narrowed his

eyes. "Either ye've fallen for the gel, or she's worth more coin to ye than the queen was offerin'."

Wraith nodded but gave no more away than that. He was conflicted himself. Faryn touched him in a way he was unaccustomed to. Och, he wanted her money, but he wanted so much more than that too.

He paced the deck of *The Avenger*, hands behind his back and gaze toward the open sea. Occasionally he glanced at his men and barked orders that really had no need of being voiced as the men were already immersed in their duties. Shouting made him feel better. But what he really needed was a fight.

"Full speed ahead!" he bellowed. The first voyage they'd made had been long, nearly a month of moons. This trip he wanted to see done in a fortnight, not thirty days, and since they'd not be making as many stops as they had before, he saw no reason why his wishes could not be made a reality.

He walked to the bow of the ship and stood, head back to look at the sky. The wind riffled through his hair as they picked up speed and spray from the salty sea splashed against his skin.

He sighed with contentment. The sea was his home, always had been, always would be. Whether he was gliding atop her fair waters or looking down at her from a window on the shore, the sea was his maiden.

Anger sliced at him as a vivid image of his childhood home flashed before his eyes. He could picture walking up the outdoor covered walkway, with arched stone ceilings and a gravel path that crunched beneath his boots. The walkway led to a doorway and beyond, winding stone steps that took him to the top of the tower. He'd lean out through one of the narrow windows, reaching his arm as far as he could, imagining droplets of water from the waves splashing up to meet his outstretched fingers. At his back were the heathered fields that lead up to the Highland mountains.

Hell and damnation!

All of it had been ripped away. His whole life taken in one night. A bloody massacre of all he knew, and his future shredded and bloody as the bodies around him.

"Cap'n?"

Startled, Wraith whipped around and growled, "What?"

Churl backed up, hands waving in defense in front of him. "Didna mean ta scare ye, Cap'n. S'only, the men be wonderin' if they can have a meal now we's out to sea."

Wraith nodded, not trusting his voice to come out sounding right through his closed throat.

"Will ye be takin' yer meal with the lady, in yer quarters?"

Again, Wraith nodded, then waved Churl away.

With a deep sigh, he made his way down to the quarterdeck and the doors leading to his cabin. But there he paused. He wanted to enter, to see Faryn again. He wanted to ask her how she fared, to discuss with her the plans for their voyage and when they landed. Wanted to gauge from her how her family would react, what amount of coin he could expect. But knowing he needed to ask those questions wasn't what stopped him. What kept him from entering the door were the other feelings creeping in, trying to take over his controlled and methodical mind. Feelings of possession, interest, desire—he dared not give voice to anything more than that.

With a curse through gritted teeth, he turned the knob on the door and slipped inside.

They'd left at dawn and now the sun blazed outside on the decks, reflecting almost blindingly from the water's surface, but despite that, inside his cabin was dark. The curtains were drawn over the few portholes and no candles were lit.

Aware of the room like he was the back of his hand, Wraith let his eyes adjust to the change in light and then looked around. Where was she?

Soft breathing and an occasional nonsensical murmur were whispered. He walked toward the bed and found her curled up under the thick plaid blankets, deep in sleep, hair fanned out like a golden halo atop her head.

He watched her. Admired her beauty. Took in her innocence. Felt himself grow drowsy with the even rise and fall of her chest.

Sleep sounded perfect. Wraith peeled off his linen shirt, had a moment where he thought being nude beside her not such a good idea but quickly tossed it overboard. They'd already made love once. What would it matter if he slept nude beside her? Hell, she herself was only dressed in one of his linen shirts.

Without another thought, he stripped down to his skin and slipped between the sheets. Lying on his side, he pulled Faryn's warm body against his length.

He ignored the quickened beat of his heart and how his breath caught in his throat. He rested a hand on her bare hip, his shirt having risen to bunch around her mid-section. Somehow, he even managed to bridle his erection, which raged hard against her soft buttocks.

Sleep was what he needed. But sleep was not what he was going to get.

CHAPTER SIX

Warmth filled her. Softness caressed her. Then hardness, stroking over her body. The scents of man and sea curled around her. She sank deeper in the blankets, completely comfortable, and relaxed into the delicious warmth and pleasure.

Faryn's eyes shot open and she jerked against a male body.

The gasp was stilled on her breath when lips claimed hers. She was rolled onto her back and a hard male body covered her. A tongue stroked along her mouth and hands roamed over her body. She should have cause to fear, but she would have recognized the kiss anywhere, and as shameful as it was, she welcomed Noir's touch.

She leaned up, deepening the kiss, and curled her

arms around his warm back, stroking over the smoothness of his flesh.

She spread her thighs beneath him, her knees at his hips, her body already slick with the need for him to sink inside her.

Noir moaned against her mouth. "Ye are a little vixen, are ye not?"

Faryn smiled and lifted her hips up until his arousal was cradled between her thighs. "I only do as my master bids me."

When Noir didn't answer right away the warmth started to desert her. Had she said something wrong? But he kissed her again, this time gently against her lips.

"Faryn, *leannan*, I dinna wish for ye to do only as I bid when we are together, like this."

She didn't know how to answer, wasn't sure what he meant by his words. "I-I dinna understand."

He pressed his forehead to hers, his hands settling on her hips. "Dinna spread your thighs for me because ye think I demand it. Do it because ye desire it. Do it because ye desire *me*."

Stunned, she lost all sense of words. She did desire him. She did want him to drive deep inside her. She needed him to touch her. But what she realized then was he needed her to tell him that. He was so accustomed to women tossing up their skirts and taking him because he wanted them to, not because they had a choice. Why did he want it to be a choice with her? At the moment she cared not why, only that he did, and that she burned with a fever so hot only he could douse it.

"Touch me," she demanded.

"Aye," he growled, and crushed his lips to hers.

He kissed her senseless while pulling his shirt from her body. His hands roamed up over her ribs to her breasts, where he teased her nipples until she writhed and begged him for more. He bent his head low, taking a nipple gently into his mouth, then scraped his teeth over it and sucked gently.

Faryn moaned and tugged at his hair. Wanting more of what he had to give. Wanting a release as sweet as the one he'd given her in Orelia's court.

"Noir, please!" she begged.

But he wouldn't let her get away that easily. "What is it, minx? What do ye want from me?"

"Oh," she gasped as his mouth went lower, his tongue circling over her navel. "Aye," she whimpered, not really sure what she was saying, only knowing that the feel of his tongue on her flesh was exquisite.

He moved lower, kissing the top of her mons and blowing gently on the nub that sparked pleasure.

She bucked her hips and shrieked, "Nay! Aye!"

He darted his tongue out to lap at her pearl.

"Mmm...*leannan*...so delicious..."

Faryn threaded her fingers through his hair and spread her thighs wider.

Wraith lapped at her bud relentlessly, until she breathed so quickly she feared she'd faint. Her legs shook and surreal pleasure radiated through her entire body. She was on the precipice, about to break apart, when he stopped and thrust his tongue deep.

She moaned and writhed as his tongue darted in and out then swirled up to circle her nub before thrusting back into her core. She pressed her hips up and down in time with his swirling, thrusting tongue. Her head fell back and forth and she moved her hands from his hair to grip at the sheets.

But as close as she was to climaxing, he wouldn't let her. Every time her body began to tremble and she was sure she'd break apart, he'd change his pace. Until she could no longer speak and her whole body shook with incomprehensible need.

He pulled his tongue from inside her and sucked her pearl into his mouth, rubbing his velvet tongue heatedly over and over the sweet nub. "Come," he growled against her in demand.

With the force of seven seas, a climax crashed through her. For a moment, she ceased to be. Life itself was nonexistent and the only thing she knew was sheer erotic pleasure as it coursed through her.

He continued to lazily lap at her tingling flesh until her tremors subsided and her legs stopped shaking.

"Ye are exquisite," he murmured. "To see ye in the

moment ye take your pleasure... I nearly came undone myself."

He pushed up onto his knees, his cock jutting out long, thick and hard.

Faryn licked her lips. She wanted to give him the same pleasure he'd given her. But she wouldn't ask, for fear he'd say nay.

"Thank ye," she said, her voice hoarse from her moaning. She pushed up into a sitting position and tucked her legs underneath her.

Faryn gulped, her mouth opening and closing as she studied his naked body. Here in the cabin, she had much more leisure to watch him, to see him, without anyone standing on the outside making her feel self-conscious. Faryn wasn't sure how to react or what to think. Sculptures and paintings had not prepared her for what jutted from between his muscled hips. Long, thick, hard. And that was only the beginning. She couldn't describe more. Her body instinctively approved—mouth watering, belly fluttering, wetness pooling between her thighs.

Oh, my... Faryn wanted to reach out and stroke the smooth, velvety sac that rest beneath the hard length of his cock. Aye, cock. She dared roll the wicked word around her mind. For cock was the only word to describe his member. No polite words would do. For his cock, was made for pleasuring. Every naughty, wanton thought she'd had since meeting Noir came to the forefront of her mind, ending with what he had done to her with the swollen flesh of his cock. What she wanted to do to him.

Her desire must have been written on her face. His lips quirked up in a smile and he nodded as if answering her unuttered question—aye, he said. Aye, he would pleasure her until her body shook like the queen's. Aye, he would take her to the pinnacle of the heavens and back down to earth again. Aye, this was happening.

"What are ye about, lass?" Wraith's eyes twinkled. And she thought for sure this rake would know of her wicked plans.

She walked her fingers up from his navel to his chest and circled over his nipples before leaning forward and licking a tiny taut tip.

He sucked in his breath and threaded a hand in her hair.

"Do ye like that?" she asked.

"Aye," he murmured.

She sucked harder on his nipple, as he'd done to her, and delighted in the short growl in the back of his throat. She tongued her way over to his other nipple, making sure it too got the same attention. As she sucked, she could hear his heart beating louder in his chest. Smug pleasure filled her, knowing she was the cause for his rapid pulse.

Taking her mouth away from his nipple, she leaned up and kissed his lips, the muskiness of her sex scented his face and flavored his tongue. She hadn't expected that but found it an extreme aphrodisiac. Her sex fluttered and the renewed pulse of desire flooded lower.

But this wasn't about her. This was about him.

She leaned lower and kissed the flat ridges of his abdomen. He sucked in his breath.

"Faryn, wait," he said lightly.

"What is it?" She had a feeling he would ask her to stop, so she didn't let her mouth leave his abdomen. Instead, she pressed kisses and licked at the flesh of his stomach and pelvis, driving him as insane as he'd driven her with his mouth.

"I—"

She wasn't about to let him protest. Before he could finish talking, she had his thick shaft in her grip and kissed the tip.

He whistled through his teeth and moaned.

She licked his flesh and stroked her hand up and down the length. She'd never sucked a man before but instinct took over.

Noir was as still as a statue, his breathing hissed between his teeth.

She didn't make him wait any longer, instead opened her mouth wide and took the tip of his cock inside. Her lips stretched wide around him and she sucked him in farther.

He groaned a sigh and pushed his hips forward, as if he'd fought an internal battle and lost.

His breathing grew harsher and he started to pull out of her mouth but she gripped his hips and thrust him back inside.

"Aye, *leannan*, aye," he murmured.

Faryn was relentless in her mission to give him the same pleasure she herself had felt.

His groans were deep and guttural, he whispered of the devil in a maiden's disguise.

She moaned against his cock as he thrust deep again. One of his hands held her hair tight. She sucked harder, keeping pace with his hips as he thrust into her mouth.

"Faryn!" he shouted, yanking himself from her, and spilling his seed on the sheet. "Blood and bones," he murmured.

She slowly rose, his gaze boring into hers, his expression one of awe. She couldn't quite read what it meant.

"Lass…I've never allowed…" His voice trailed off and he pulled her against him, fell to the bed, her head on his chest, their legs entwined. "I've never allowed any woman to put her mouth on me."

Faryn was shocked at his words.

"Why?" she whispered.

"It is about control for me," he stated flatly. "When your mouth was on me…I lost all control. I let ye lead me to salvation."

Faryn chuckled. "I wouldna exactly call it salvation."

Noir laughed too and kissed her on top of her head. "Sounds odd, aye, but believe me, it is a salvation of sorts."

"I am glad I can bring ye that."

"Me too. I've lived in the dark for so long, and the moment ye first raised your eyes to mine a warmth settled inside me. I fear..." He trailed off again, as if his emotions were too strong to discuss and he was revealing to her things he'd probably never told another soul.

Their gazes met and held. Faryn's heart clenched. Why was he having this effect on her?

A knock at the door interrupted their locked gazes, giving them both a reprieve from whatever was building between them.

Wraith tossed the blankets back on top of her and pulled on his breeches.

"Enter," he growled.

The door opened to several of the captain's servants, who brought in trays of food, a jug of wine and serving dishes. With a glare from Wraith, they did not glance toward the bed where she lay nude beneath the blankets and still trembling. Instead, they kept their eyes on their work and then hurried to leave.

"Shall we dine, *leannan*?" Wraith said, his lips curved in invitation. "Or did ye have your fill on the first course?"

Faryn's cheeks flamed with embarrassment.

"Nay, Captain, I am still starving." She flipped back the covers, aware that she was showing him all of her, then placed her feet on the floor. A moment's questions about how she could be so bold with this man, and how her family would surely die of shame, flashed in her mind before she shoved them away.

She sauntered to the table, her stomach growling, and her body yearning for a man she felt like she'd known forever.

CHAPTER SEVEN

Storm clouds raged above and the ship rocked back and forth. Winds blew the sails this way and that and waves crashed against the hull.

Faryn was safe and warm in Wraith's cabin from the tempest that beat the outside of the ship, but inside her mind turmoil brewed. In fact, the week they'd spent aboard ship had torn her apart inside. She was falling deeply for the rakehell pirate captain and wasn't quite sure what she could do about it. Or how to react to such strong emotions.

What could she do? He would return her to her home. She would have to marry Lord Bréagadóir and suffer for the rest of her days—which would most likely be numbered. He'd made it clear he did not truly wish to marry her but would do so for her parents' sake and the money they would pay him.

And Wraith would go back to being a dread pirate on the open seas.

A chill swept over her despite being curled up beneath thick blankets. Dear heavens, she'd spent more time in bed in the last week than she had her entire life. Living aboard ship as the guest of Captain Noir certainly had its benefits. He catered to her every need—not only sensually but in everything else as well. And oddly enough, he seemed to gain satisfaction from it. He was genuinely pleased to be in her company, although at times she could see he struggled with something.

She wanted to ask what it was but she was afraid he was only disgusted with himself for treating her so well, so she did not.

Face reality, Faryn, he is only using ye for coin.

She frowned at nothing and climbed from bed, wrapping the thick wool blanket around her shoulders. She made her way to the porthole and gazed outside at the storm. Lightning streaked across the sky and seconds later a loud boom of thunder hit. She had a sudden urge to leave the cabin, one she hadn't had since boarding, but now she wanted to. She wanted to see the men at work, wanted to feel the rain on her face. Maybe it would help to wash away some of the shame she was beginning to feel at her behavior—at having not noticed before, or refusing to see, that the captain was only using her.

Just thinking about it brought tears to her eyes.

What a fool she was! What did she think? That the captain would fall madly in love with her and sail her around the world while they pirated together?

She could not be part of such dealings, and he would never fall in love with her. Hadn't her parents always told her she was foolish and childish for wishing for love in the first place? Her father had constantly lectured about how a person made their own fate, that emotions had little play in it.

For her father, how true those words were. He'd offered her no comfort when she'd been ill used the previous spring. He'd only paid a man to take her off his hands. Her fiancé was the worst sort of man there could be.

In fact, being abducted now seemed like a blessing…

∼

FIGHTING foul weather on Mother Nature's open seas was a worse battle than if they'd been boarded by enemy pirates.

Already one crewman was tossed overboard with the force of the winds. The men had tried to throw him a line while at the same time trying to regain control of the ship. They won the ship but lost the man.

Wraith's head pounded.

He wanted nothing more than to go to his cabin

and slip his arms around the beautiful woman who awaited him. To forget the ship, his crew and this hellacious storm.

He ducked suddenly as rigging went flying overhead.

"Churl!" he shouted.

"On it!" his mate hurled back.

The crew scurried around him as the storm picked up wind and took hold of his ship again.

Faryn took root in his mind again, the thought of her curvy hips, round bouncing breasts, taut nipples, wet, hot...

A waved crashed over the side, splashing him.

He frowned. Each time he thought of the woman below, something happened. Spirits ran rampant on the sea. Ghost ships, specters, spirits controlling the waters, the weather. Was the universe trying to tell him something?

A thick rope lashed out from seemingly nowhere and whipped him in the arm.

"Damn!" he hissed in pain, somewhat relieved to see no damage had been done.

Gooseflesh rose along his limbs. Someone *was* trying to tell him something. Was not the ship's name *The Avenger* for a reason? He was letting his whole purpose for saving her, his whole purpose for living, slip away.

Problem was, part of him wanted it to slip away. More than a part of him wanted to live a life with

Faryn. Have her to wife. Raise a few bairns he could bounce on his knee.

All rubbish! Nothing would ever come of his foolish fantasies. He had revenge to play out. She was the key.

But dammit if he wasn't going to continue to enjoy her while the voyage lasted, key or not, foolish dreams or nay.

∼

A SHARP RAP on the door pulled Faryn from her reverie as she'd stared out the porthole. Making sure she was covered as much by the blanket as she could reasonably manage and appeared somewhat decent—despite her lack of clothing—she called out, "Enter."

The door opened and in hobbled several crewmen carrying a copper tub, followed by numerous buckets of warm, steaming water.

"A bath?" she asked.

"Aye, his cap'nship wants a bath fer hisself," one of the crew stated while pouring a steaming bucket into the tub.

Oh, she hoped he'd allow her to use the tub when he was finished. She looked toward the water bowl and basin she'd been using, filled only with cold water. As soon as the crew left, she would fill the basin with warm water from the captain's tub. Even if she couldn't submerge herself in a hot, delicious bath, she would at least have warm water to wash her face and body with.

"Now, dinna ye be usin' his cap'nship's bath!" the insolent Churl warned. "He dinna like no second handlins' of the water."

She rolled her eyes and turned away in a huff.

The door closed quietly as the last of them left and still she refused to look at the copper tub. As much as she'd decided she would put warm water into her own small water bowl, rebellion rose inside her. He didn't like to be second to wash. Well then, those nefarious crewmen would have to refill the tub for him, because like it or not, she was getting in!

Before she could turn around, there came a loud splash. She gasped and whirled to see that the captain had already plunged into the steamy water, and she'd not even heard him come in. He must have slipped in before Churl finished closing the door.

Noir laid his head back and glanced over at her. "Join me?" he drawled. His lips were curved in that devilish teasing way he had and she realized the crew had only been toying with her.

"I would love to."

She dropped the blanket and shucked off her shirt before sauntering toward the tub. She loved the way the captain's eyes roved over her body as she made her way there. Made her feel like a goddess.

He held out a hand to her and she lifted a leg up

and over the side. Holding on to her hips, he settled her between his thighs. His cock was hard and pressed against the small of her back, and a frisson of need wound its way from her breasts to her core.

"Have I told ye today what a vision ye make?" he murmured against her neck as he moved her hair out of his way.

"Only five or six times," she laughed softly.

"Ye are...but as beautiful as ye are, my love, ye smell ungodly."

She gasped at him and turned around to slap at him for saying such a thing but he only laughed and ducked. Only realizing too late, that he'd called her *my love*. Had he meant it?

"Ye are no flowerbed yourself, Captain."

"Indeed, rutting as much as we have would certainly make one smell a bit wretched."

They laughed and teased each other some more, comparing scents with animals, barns and other awful situations until tears filled their eyes.

"I'd have still fu—" he stopped himself short, "make love to ye if ye asked."

She rolled her eyes and laughed as he tickled her ribs. "No need to sweeten your words for my womanly ears, Noir. I've enjoyed every minute of our rutting."

"Now onto the bathing, so we might rut some more."

He washed her back, her breasts, her most sensitive parts, stopping a moment to stroke her until she writhed against him. But he stopped just short of letting her climax. He continued down to her toes, massaging sweet-scented soap into the soles of her feet. He poured warm water over her hair and kneaded her scalp until she couldn't keep her eyes open from the pleasure of it.

When he was finished, she turned around to kneel between his legs and rubbed soap into his chest, returning the intimate gesture of washing.

She lathered up his arms, marveling in the feel of the sinewy muscles beneath his flesh. She washed his face, his neck, his shoulders and down over his back. He too closed his eyes as she washed his hair and then she moved down his legs, to his feet, purposefully ignoring his hard cock, which peeked above the froth-covered water.

But she didn't make him wait too long. Soon enough she stroked a soapy hand over his thick length, up and down, up and down until he grew hard as granite in her hand. Even sitting in the water, she grew slick with the need to slide him inside her, but she wasn't sure how it would work. He took up nearly the whole tub. She couldn't straddle his lap.

He must have seen her mind working, as his eyes darkened and he caught her mouth in a demanding kiss. His tongue delved deep, his hands gripped her hips, her breasts. He plucked at her nipples until she moaned into his mouth.

"Turn around," he whispered.

She did as he asked, turning on her knees, her hands holding the rim of the rub. He knelt behind her, his thick arousal probing her entrance. A sudden thrill rushed through her. He pressed against her again. Desire sparked through her and every inch of her flesh tingled. She rolled her hips back, wanting him to push inside her. He thrust hard.

She gasped aloud as he worked her body. One hand around front, caressing her nipples then sliding lower to thumb over her nub.

Her body felt on fire as pleasure and excitement swirled up and down her limbs and to her center and back again. She moaned nearly constantly and Wraith grunted and moaned behind her.

He pumped faster, harder still, water sloshing over the sides and the sound of their wet bodies joining echoed in the room.

Just when she thought she couldn't take any more, her body had mercy on her. She climaxed with uncontrollable shudders, her womb contracting, body arching, head thrown back. A guttural, feral moan escaped her lips and along with her Wraith too shuddered, pulling out, his warm liquid finish dripping over the skin of her behind.

Neither one of them moved for several moments and then a warm wet cloth stroked across her buttocks as her pirate captain cleaned away their lovemaking.

When he was finished he pulled her from the tub and gently dried the water from her bottom to the top with a linen towel, his own body still covered in droplets that fell in rivulets over the curves and contours of his muscles. After toweling her hair, he gazed into her eyes and stroked her cheek. A tiny smile curved his lips.

"Thank ye, *leannan*," he whispered and brushed a kiss on her lips.

A booming sounded in the distance and the romantic connection was lost. Both whipped their heads toward the porthole and Wraith made it to the wall in two strides to peer out.

"What is it?" Faryn came up beside him but couldn't see past his broad shoulders.

"Ship." His voice held no emotion but the clenching of his jaw gave way that it affected him.

"Friend or foe?" she asked, hoping against all hope it was friendly.

"My friends dinna shoot cannons at me, lass." He chuckled bitterly. "That is unless I deserve it, and I assure ye, I have not vexed any of my friends of late."

She nodded, swallowed hard, remained silent.

Shouts from above and the pounding of running feet echoed in the captain's quarters.

A crewman burst through the door and Faryn clutched her towel tightly to her body.

"Cap'n! Pardon me, my lady," he bowed, but then returned his attention to Wraith. *"The Avenger's under attack!"*

Beside her, she sensed rather than saw every muscle in Wraith's body tighten. Her heart constricted and her stomach plummeted.

Today she would die.

CHAPTER EIGHT

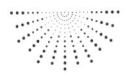

"Stay here," Wraith ordered.

Faryn nodded, her throat tight from fear. She eyed him warily as he plunged his muscled legs into breeches, stuffed his feet in boots. He didn't bother to put on a shirt but placed his plaid belt at his hips, a gun on one side followed by knives, which made their way around his belt to the other side. A sword loop remained empty at his hip, as he held the long deadly weapon within his hand. He tossed a look back at her, one of longing, before heading to the door.

She opened her mouth to speak and held out a hand imploringly, but was unsure of what to say. "Captain," squeaked out.

He turned to face her and, most likely seeing the fear and vulnerability etched on her face, turned around and in just a few strides made his way to her.

He threaded fingers through her hair with one hand and pulled her face to his.

"Dinna worry so, my love. I am the dread pirate Captain Wraith Noir." He said no more, only captured her lips with his in a demanding, erotic kiss. One that broached no argument, one that said how powerful he was and that when he finished with his enemies, he would come back to claim her.

When he pulled away, leaving her bemused, she gazed at his storm cloud eyes with glazed ones of her own. "Be careful, Wraith. Come back to me."

He nodded once, his lips curved in a wicked smile and then he was gone.

She stood in the empty room, cold, alone, scared, and listened to the sounds of bloodshed being committed above, to the sounds of the dying and a faint triumphant calling, which she hoped was Wraith as he cut through the lines to regain control of his ship.

Wraith wielded his sword at the men who poured onto his ship like ants on a forgotten sweet mincemeat pie.

But his ship was no piece of pie, and was not forgotten either. His men and he would fight to the death to keep the ship. For this was his life, and the cargo it held more precious to him than anything else—the lass and his ticket to freedom.

The men they fought were not other pirates. Although the men were not dressed in uniform or in particularly lavish attire, their weapons looked like they belonged to a military faction, although he had the distinct impression they'd not been trained to use them. He felled one man after another until he came upon a gentleman who was dressed in noble attire. Sweat covered the man's brow as he fought for his life against Churl.

He was pleased to see that most of his own men had gotten the upper hand and had either sent the attackers to their maker or tied them up as prisoners.

Noir stood beyond the circle Churl and the gentleman were making with their parried dance, arms crossed over his chest, fist swinging out every once in a while to knock a man who attacked him unconscious with the butt of his sword.

Watching Churl fight was a pleasure. The man had a unique style of bringing his prey in, letting them think they had the upper hand and then springing an unseen hit on them.

He laughed aloud when Churl kicked the man in his ballocks, causing him to fall to his knees. The gentleman cursed and turned his eyes on Wraith.

"Ye the captain?" he asked, his accent distinctly Irish, at the same time as Churl prepared to butt him on the back of the head.

Wraith held up his hand and to Churl said, "Hold, man, let me speak to him."

Churl nodded and snickered, giving the man a

kick in the ribs instead. The gentleman doubled over, holding his belly.

"I am the captain of this ship. What the bloody hell do ye think ye're doing attacking us? Are ye mad, man?"

The man looked up, blood sweating into his eye from a cut on his brow. "Ye have something of mine, I believe." His lip curled into a mean smile showing dark rotted teeth and a few spaces where teeth should have been. For all his noble clothes and weaponry he looked as though he drank a cask of wine an hour and never once cleaned his teeth with a bit of root or the like. There was something oddly familiar about the man, too. "And I want it back."

Wraith laughed cruelly, sheathed his sword and walked forward, stalking the man. "Ye think to become a pirate yourself then, mate?"

"I am a peer and ye shall address me so," the man sneered.

Wraith shot forward, jolting the man. He grabbed him by his collar and lifted him up to face Wraith eye to eye. "A peer? On the open seas there are no peers, and here I am king."

The man actually shuddered but quickly pulled himself to rights. "I shall require my betrothed. She is mine. Sold to me by her parents."

"Betrothed ye say? I dinna think so."

"I've already had it confirmed by one of your

men, Captain Noir. Lady Faryn is mine!" Spittle flew from the man's mouth.

Wraith ignored the spittle. Ignored the red-faced man he held in the air. All he could think of was the beauty below stairs. How much she meant to him, and that he couldn't possibly lose her. Especially not to this man. Not to this monster, with his blackened teeth and foul breath. His sweating, stinking body. His evilness that radiated off him in waves. She'd never make it.

Finally, Wraith smiled. It was a deadly smile. Cold, unforgiving. "Funny thing is, mate," he said, dropping the man back on the deck, "I bought her myself. And I dinna take kindly to others stealing what is mine."

The man on the deck let out a desperate growl and lunged at Wraith, a dirk that had before been concealed glinting in the sunlight. He jabbed at Wraith with manic intent. The man was mad. No matter how Wraith blocked the blows, here the wretch came back, cutting wherever he could and shouting vile curses. Even when Wraith was able to wrestle him to the ground, the bastard wouldn't give up. He pulled a pistol from his belt and held it to Noir's belly, every intention to pull the trigger. Enough was enough. With one click of his skull and crossbones ring, Wraith put an end to the assault and sliced the man's neck from ear to ear.

The maggot fell to the deck again, clutching at

his severed neck, blood spilling from between his fingers.

"Shouldna have lunged at me, mate. 'Tis a shame, since I fully intended to keep ye alive and negotiate." Wraith wiped the thin blade on the man's coat and then clicked the button to retract it back into his ring, watching the dying man look at his ring. "Thing comes in handy in a pinch. Didna even catch your name to ask the lass if ye were her man. Could be I dinna have Lady Faryn onboard and my man was mistaken. Could be ye died for nothing."

Wraith left the man to die with the thought of his vile mistakes the last on his dying mind.

"We take no prisoners! Toss 'em to the sharks. Those who make it back to their ship are saved, those who dinna become feed for the fishes."

His men shouted and cheered, happy to toss their prisoners overboard. He could hear the splashing with subtle differences. The splashing of those who could swim making a mad dash for their ship, and those who could not swim as they thrashed for their lives.

Life had made him a bitter man.

Now to find out whom exactly his new bounty piece was. Pleasure had to now be at an end.

CHAPTER NINE

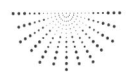

He opened the door and let it bang sharply against the wall. Faryn jerked from her place at the porthole where she peered out onto the expansive sea.

"Men died today, lass. 'Tis your doing." He scowled at her.

She scowled back, arms spread wide. "My doing?" Her voice was high-pitched, exasperated. "How in the world can ye see fit to blame your pirating ways on me?"

"'Tis quite easy actually. They came looking for ye."

"For me?" Her face lost all color and she sank to the floor in a puddle of white linen.

"Aye. Never got the maggot's name, but he had blackened teeth and claimed ye for his bride."

"Nay," she whispered, shaking her head. "Nay, it canna be!"

"Are ye calling me a liar?"

She looked up sharply, tears glistening in her eyes, making his heart lurch. He longed to reach out and hold her, tell her everything would be all right, but he couldn't. He needed answers.

"Tell me everything," he demanded.

"I dinna know where to start." Her voice was so small and vulnerable. Her hands clutched at the linen in a grip so tight her knuckles were white.

"Start with his name, who he was to ye."

"His name is Lord Bréagadóir."

The name meant nothing to him. "He says ye were sold to him. What does he mean by that?"

Her face flushed red and she looked down at the wooden planks of the floor. "My parents gave him a large dowry to take me off their hands as no other man would have me." She looked up, her wide eyes glassy with unshed tears. But he was struck more with the defiance he saw. She was a fighter and would not cower easily. "But ye see, when ye took me from the shore that night, he had not yet received the coin. Bréagadóir is in deep with his creditors. My father promised him a lot of gold if he would only look the other way when there was no blood on the sheets on our wedding night. If he didna get the coin, he would have been dead as the creditors would have killed him or sent him to debtor's prison." Her gaze flicked around the room, settling on anything but him. "Bréagadóir would have killed me, I am sure. He all but promised once he got what he wanted, he'd be done with me."

"Who is your father?"

"My father is Henry, Baron Claneford."

Wraith drew a deep breath, excitement coursing through his veins. He'd known her father was a powerful man, but not how close he actually was to getting his future back. The baron would be instrumental in his freedom.

"Was Bréagadóir the man who took your maidenhead?" The *bastard*. He could kill him all over again.

"Nay," she said, shaking her head, her long blonde locks bobbing against her bare shoulders. "I was naïve. Fancied myself in love and let a handsome young groom seduce me. He promised to take me away, to marry me."

Wraith was affronted that any man would lead her astray—betray her, and so openly and on her father's own land but then again, he'd kidnapped her… though unknowingly. Women were so vulnerable. It made him angry, so angry in fact his blood heated with hatred. How many of the women he'd delivered to Orelia had been just like Faryn? And hadn't he himself bargained for her from the vulgar queen—yet again taking her control away?

Disgust roiled in his belly.

"Had ye no chaperone?" he asked absentmindedly, not sure why he'd even asked in the first place.

"My father chose the groom as my escort when I rode, as my maid was quite old. Francis had ample opportunity to woo me and he took advantage of that... Although I suppose I am to blame for most of it."

"Nay, never, Faryn. Your father should have had more control over his men, and Francis should never have used ye in such a way. Was he punished?"

Faryn shook her head, her eyes downcast. "Nay, he disappeared the next morning. My maid found us nude in my bed and she screamed, calling for my father and the guards. Francis fought his way out and I never saw him again."

Wraith nodded. He thought of Bréagadóir, wondered if the man had actually been behind Faryn's fall from grace. He could have planned the whole thing—paid the man to seduce her. It could have all been a ruse to gain her father's money. Then it hit him. Wraith knew instantly why the man had seemed familiar to him. He'd seen him before. Dealt with him before. The eve of his family's murder. Bréagadóir had come to the castle his mother had inherited on the coast of Ireland, but he'd been dressed as a beggar. He'd begged food and shelter and they'd let him sleep in the stables. Must have been how the murderers had gained access—he'd opened the gates. Let them in.

Whoever it was had been bent on seeing that the castle remained in Irish hands, not Scottish. But there was no way that Bréagadóir wasn't the mastermind. Nay, he wasn't that smart—and he still had all of his fingers.

"Come, I have to show ye something."

Wraith took an iron key from behind a plank of wood that had blended seamlessly with the wall of his cabin. He was still shirtless and Faryn found herself breathing hard, her heart erratic at not just his near nakedness, but at what she'd revealed, how he'd reacted.

She'd seen the anger simmering inside him. And she was both intrigued and excited that he would be angry on her behalf.

He took the key to a chest beside his desk and unlocked the padlock, an audible click echoing in the silence. With steady hands, he lifted the lid, which made a loud creaking noise, as if rarely used. She half expected to see a skeleton or even the heart of Davy Jones pop out from the depths but instead he lifted a large package wrapped in dark green velvet.

He took it to the table where they'd eaten only that morning and set it down.

"This is proof." A light came into his eyes.

She furrowed her brow. "Proof?"

"Faryn, lass, I have not been altogether honest with ye. My name is…"

She held up her hand, not sure if she wanted to hear what he had to say. "Wait! Dinna!"

His face fell. "Why?" His voice sounded far-off, choked.

She came forward and took his hand in hers. "Wraith, I've come to know ye over the last week and I know ye to be a good man. A pirate ye may be, but this is where ye keep your treasure." She tapped his chest. "Ye have a heart of gold. I can see in your eyes the depths of your soul and I've grown...fond of it. Dinna take that away."

A smile curved his lips and he bent to kiss her knuckles.

"I too have grown to care for ye, *leannan*. Let me show ye who I really am. Let me tell ye why I took an interest in ye, so ye dinna think I want ye only for a lover's tryst. Ye mean so much more to me than that."

His words meant more to her than she could have ever realized. They meant the odd relationship they'd forged was not one-sided. Not something she'd made up in her mind. He cared for her. Perhaps a future was possible... "If ye promise it will not ruin what we have, then go on."

"I promise." He pulled her against him, kissed her softly on the lips, the heat of his body sinking into her. Warming her fear, making her feel safe and...at home. Something she hadn't felt for a long time.

When he finally pulled away, she was only half

interested in what evidence lay beneath the velvet and instead wanted only to take him by the hand and lead him to the bed they'd shared.

With reluctance, she stepped back, as it was evident how very important Wraith believed it was to share with her his past and his proof.

"I am Scottish borne, my father a powerful man in Scotland. But my mother was Irish. And when he married her, he inherited her father's title upon his death. A title that now should be mine. My father was the late Earl of Drohgard—overlord of your father."

Faryn gasped, her hand coming to her throat, and she stepped back, nearly tripping on the overflowing linens she still had wrapped about her. "Nay! Nay!" She shook her head, fear suddenly coming over her. He was more than a pirate. He was a cold-blooded murderer. Had she read him completely wrong?

She turned and raced for the door of the cabin, not caring that the ship's crew would see her in such a state. She had to get away from him, for he could only wish to reveal himself, the heinous and satanic man that he was, in order to kill her too! Stories of the murders of his family from a few years ago came to mind. Her father's description of the scene flashed before her eyes. So much blood. Severed limbs. Broken bodies. Even the children. All murdered. And the eldest son, she couldn't remember his name, but nevertheless he was gone.

Run away from his deeds. That was *he*, her Noir a murderer.

"Faryn!" he bellowed and then was on top of her, pinning her down.

She thrashed against him. "Nay! Dinna kill me. Please, I know nothing. I dinna know ye, ye can let me go. I swear I will tell no one. Please!"

"Faryn, listen! God, woman! Have ye no wits? I am innocent. *Innocent*. Someone has framed me."

His frantic words struck a chord in her. Innocent? "Ye didna murder them?" she asked meekly.

"Never. I loved my family. I love them still. 'Tis why I must get back to Ireland. I must clear my name. I have proof." He pointed at the velvet package again. "I was forced to leave. I became a pirate to support myself and my need for revenge. Joined the Devils of the Deep, a pirate brethren, and they became my new family. I searched all this time for evidence to clear my name. And now I've gathered enough. But the king will not just offer me an audience, despite his having known my father, I will have to bribe him to see me. I've amassed a small fortune but the bounty—the daughter of a lord is well worth her weight in gold. 'Tis why I bargained for ye. Ye shall help me. And now that I know who your father is, he can help me, too, for he knows me. He knows I wouldna have killed my family. He can vouch for me."

Faryn nodded, although she wasn't sure that her

father would do any such thing. In fact, the more she thought of it, the more she realized he'd probably written her off completely. Wasn't that apparent in the fact that he had not accompanied Bréagadóir in the search to find her? Or perhaps he was covering the lands and Bréagadóir had agreed to scour the seas.

Aye, that must be it. Her father must be searching all of Ireland for her.

"Show me." She pointed to the package and, taking her hand, Wraith led her to the table.

He squeezed her hand and then let it go, and while she was still scared, she felt the absence of his touch immensely.

With measured movements, he unwrapped the velvet, revealing a small pile of items and papers.

He first showed her a letter. "This is a letter one of my spies intercepted. It is from the murderer—although he hasna signed it—but he confesses to an accomplice of their deeds and how he plans to petition the king for the earldom—my father's titles and estates—my rightful inheritance."

"Did he ever gain such?" She couldn't recall if there had been a new earl or not, though she had never really paid attention to those things, if she was privy to the information, which wasn't very often. After she'd been sorely used and heartbroken, which was shortly before the murders, she kept to herself, and then she was betrothed to Bréagadóir and soon captured by Wraith.

"Not as of yet. The Lord Chancellor, Viscount Loftford, holds the estates in the name of the king, taking the money for himself. He says he holds it until I am found." Wraith stopped talking for a short moment and stared off into the distance. "Loftford was a friend of a sort of my father's. I think he doesna believe me capable of the heinous crimes I've been charged with, but so many have placed blame on me. I believe he waits for me to return to tell him myself what happened."

"And now ye shall."

He nodded and then picked up the next item, a jeweled belt. "This was my father's. He had it on him when he was murdered, but when his body was found the belt was missing. The belt was being sold at a market, and when I questioned the man who sold it, he described the man who had sold it to him. A witness. Ye can still see the blood dried between the links here." He pointed to a dark reddish-brown stain between several jeweled links.

Faryn nodded, feeling her stomach recoil.

"And this last bit is the *piece de résistance*." He tapped another velvet-wrapped object. "But I canna show ye what it is."

Faryn frowned. "Why ever not?"

"I have never shown anyone before. I am…" he trailed off, his face suddenly looking vulnerable.

"Mayhap this is all too much for ye. Ye've already bared your soul to me."

She squared her shoulders, and with as much strength as she could muster covered in only a linen sheet, she spoke. "Wraith, I am not a child. I have been through more than most women I know, and I've come out on top, and strong." Now she told him, only because of what he'd said, and because she wanted him to think she could handle whatever it was that lay hidden beneath the fabric. "Show me. I will not shy away from it."

He nodded, his mouth set in a grim line. "I took this myself from the scene, when I fought one of the attackers." He unfolded the cloth carefully, revealing a gold ring with a large ruby. "I will have my vengeance on the man who did this."

The way the ring sat on the linen, the crest faced away from her and she could not read the tiny inscription along its side.

"A ring," she said, unable to state more than the obvious.

"Aye. The ring of the man who killed my father—I wrenched it from his finger as we fought." With the tip of his finger, he rolled the ring so she could see the crest.

It was then Faryn lost her balance and her struggle to remain calm. She turned away quickly, gasping for air. But it was no use. She ran to the nearest chamber pot and vomited. Just when she thought her stomach was good and empty, she heaved again.

"I knew I shouldna have shared this with ye, it is too much after your confession," Wraith muttered as he gently pulled her hair back and rubbed a wet cloth on her neck and face. "Forgive me."

But she shook her head. It wasn't that he'd shared the information with her that disturbed her, but the ring.

A ring she'd seen many times before and on a man she would never have guessed could be capable of murder. A man who in her turmoil over the last few years, she hadn't noticed was missing his prized family heirloom.

Her father.

CHAPTER TEN

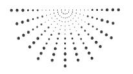

Wraith was called to the stern while Faryn splashed water on her face.

Her whole body was numb, yet it tingled all the same, and every time she recollected the ring, her stomach protested. But seeing as how she'd already emptied it, there was nothing left for her to toss up. So she sat, huddled in a ball on the corner of the bed, against the wall, totally in limbo.

How could she bring Wraith to her family now? Knowing that her own father had been the one to murder his family…

She hoped and prayed they never set foot in Ireland after tonight's discovery.

Her father would try to kill Wraith. To finish the job he'd started so many years ago. This had to be a mistake. Someone must have stolen the ring… But even as she thought it, she could recall witnessing her father on the battlefield, seeing him be ruthless at a meeting of lords. If he felt at all threatened, he was merciless.

And once Wraith found out who the ring belonged to, he would never look at her the same again. Her father was a cold-blooded murderer. Wraith would unknowingly resent her, put the blame for his family's death on her.

She squeezed her eyes tightly shut and took a few long, slow breaths. What was she to do? She didn't want to leave Wraith. She didn't want him to get hurt or worse. She didn't want him to hate her... With that, she came to a startling realization, a strong tug in her chest and a lump in her throat. She'd come to love him. For all they'd only known each other a short time, he was the only man who'd ever made her feel special, important, cared for.

She couldn't let him walk to his own death. She had to stop him.

Was it best to steer him away? But how could she? When he discovered the crest was her family's, there would be no stopping him. He knew who her father was, where her family's keep was located.

If only she could convince him to go to the Lord Chancellor of Ireland first. Viscount Loftford spoke for the King of England, which was also the King of Ireland. He would be able to resolve this matter.

Aye! That was it. She would convince him to go to the Lord Chancellor first, before taking her home

—except she didn't even *want* to go home, now. Not ever. But that was beside the point. Right now, she had to figure out a way to save Wraith. Viscount Loftford was the key. While there, she would seek an audience with the man himself. She would confess that she recognized the ring. She would tell him of her father's deeds. And then she would drop to her knees in front of Wraith, beg his forgiveness, swear to him she hadn't known.

And pray pray *pray* he believed her and took mercy on her.

Wraith stood at the helm of his ship and peered through the telescope at the far-off shore of Ireland. Clew Bay was their destination. A port town that was rife with pirate activity, but there was no need to draw attention to themselves. When the sun set, they would lay anchor at sea, and just before dawn, sail into the northern beach of Keel, and from there make their way south on horseback to from the west coast to the east coast, and Dublin. 'Twas necessary for his own safety and that of his crew that they not dock close to where he needed to meet the Lord Chancellor. Most of his crew would remain aboard the ship, and if he did not return within the allotted time, they would retreat.

Already they'd taken down his pirate's flag and replaced it with a regular sail in case they were spotted. There was nothing to distinguish them as friend or foe, and he hoped that they ran into no other ships before laying anchor.

One more night with Faryn.

That was all he had until he returned her to her family and made his way to the Lord Chancellor. He'd spent years at sea, dreaming of the moment he could bring justice for his parents and himself to light. And here it was.

So, why did it feel like a knife twisting in his gut? He rubbed the imaginary soreness and indicated to Churl that he was going below deck to his quarters. "Let the men be merry tonight, for just before dawn we dock and our true adventure begins."

He descended the ladder and paused outside his cabin door. How would he say goodbye to her?

Was he becoming such a dim-witted fancy pants? Never had a woman made him feel this way before. He refused to put his feelings into words. He shook his head and opened the door.

Faryn sat on the bed, curled up into a little ball, looking lost and forlorn.

Perhaps the lass needed a bit of what he sought.

"A glass of whisky?" he asked, walking to an armoire that housed drinking cups and liquor.

Her eyes lit up at his suggestion. "Aye, please. I've only ever had wine and ale before."

He chuckled a bit at the excitement in her voice. "Drink it slowly. 'Twill warm your belly and soothe your mind." He pulled out the whisky and poured a healthy portion for himself and a smaller splash for Faryn. He handed her the cup. "To us." A sweet smile curved her lips, making him want to take her in his arms and kiss her. Not just any kiss but the kiss of a man in lov—

He shook his head and slugged back the entire cup of spirits, letting it burn its way down his throat until it sat hot in his belly.

She too slugged back the liquor, and screwed up her face with distaste. "Whew!" she breathed. "I had thought ye sipped it."

Wraith let his head fall back with a laugh that burst from the center of his being. The little imp had watched him chug his drink and followed suit, thinking that the proper way.

"What? Was I not supposed to?" Her nose wrinkled and she looked genuinely concerned.

He only laughed harder.

She stood and her hands went to her hips, her brows furrowed. "Captain, I demand ye tell me what ye're laughing at!"

"Ye, *leannan*. Ye are exactly the balm this hard-hearted pirate needs."

He did kiss her then, his mouth covering hers, his tongue sweeping in to claim her for his own. She tasted of sweet whisky and femininity. He swept her up into his arms and carried her to the bed, where he laid her, before coming down on top of her, not breaking their kiss.

Faryn sighed against him, arms circling around him. Ever willing and excited to make love to him. It only made his heart swell thicker in his chest. Slowly he tugged the white linen shirt she wore from her body, before he caressed her breasts and nipples, letting his mouth fall where his hands had splayed. She tensed and arched against him as he nuzzled her breasts, sucking a nipple into his mouth, teasing it with his tongue, grazing it with his teeth.

She explored his skin and he trembled beneath her touch, loving the way she boldly and tenderly caressed him. Tugging at his belt, she somehow managed to remove it and then shimmied his breeches down over his thighs and he kicked them to the floor.

She nipped at his neck, licked his lobe and pressed kisses to his face.

"This is our last night together," he said breathily, and kissed her lightly on the lips. Their bodies molded together so perfectly. If he could, he would never leave the bed, content to lie in the warmth of her arms forever.

"Let it not be our last night," she murmured, bringing a knee up and caressing his hip with her calf, her toes trailing down his thigh.

"There is no other way," he said, rubbing a hand over her silky, lithe leg.

"Aye, there is." She brought up her other knee and

lifted her hips, cradling his hard cock against her sex.

"How?" he asked, pressing his own hips forward until the tip of his arousal pushed into her opening.

"Oh," she moaned and lifted her hips more, her body begging for him to move deeper.

"Tell me, Faryn, tell me. I want to know how I can keep ye forever." He pressed his forehead to hers and drove all the way inside her.

"Aye, keep me forever," she whispered, pressing hot kisses to his shoulder and neck. She rocked her hips up and down, her fingers scratching down his back. "If we could only stay like this."

"Oh aye," he moaned, pulling out and plunging deep.

Her moans increased, and talking ceased as she succumbed to his lovemaking. He drove in again and again, lifting her buttocks to sink in deeper still.

Soon the sounds of their moans and the creaking of the bed echoed in the cabin.

And then the final culmination, as her body shook and she arched her back, head falling back, and he too let go, releasing deep inside her.

When their breathing had returned to normal, Wraith lay down on his back and pulled Faryn to lie atop him so he could stroke her silky hair.

"Ye didna tell me," he said.

"Tell ye what?" she asked, her voice warm like that of a sated woman.

"How can we make tonight last forever?"

She nodded, her cheek rubbing against his chest. "Let us go to the Lord Chancellor first, and not my father. Then we can at least prolong our parting. That is, unless…" But she trailed off.

He stiffened. Would she reject him now? How he desperately needed her! His heart ached with the thought of not being near her. "Unless what?"

"Unless there is a way to never take me home again. I could stay with ye. Here. On the ship."

The thought had not occurred to him to keep her forever. Once they'd made his statements to the Lord Chancellor and cleared his name—he wasn't sure what he was going to do. He'd never made plans that far in advance. Over the years, it had only been that he needed to seek revenge on those who'd destroyed him.

"Do ye not wish to return home?"

She looked up at him, confused. "Wraith, my family has sold me to the only man who would have me—a vicious and vile man. Who thankfully ye have dispatched." She crossed herself. "I should never wish him dead but I canna help it, as he for sure would have seen me returned to the earth. They will only sell me again and this time to someone worse. I will not return."

He didn't want to promise her anything, because he wasn't sure if even with his proof the Lord Chancellor would believe him, and that if he did believe

Wraith, that he would return his lands. It could be that Viscount Loftford enjoyed taking the tariffs from his land, that they lined his coffers quite well and he would rather see Wraith convicted and guillotined than return what was rightfully his.

If such were the case, Wraith wasn't sure he'd be able to escape…at least not with a pulse.

"We shall travel together and see what the Lord Chancellor declares upon seeing my proof of innocence. I canna promise ye anything until then, Faryn. But know this, I would have ye with me always, and I willna take ye to your father's home if 'tis your wish."

CHAPTER ELEVEN

The cabin was dark, except for a light orange-pink light that shafted through the porthole to dance on the opposite wall—dusk. Faryn sat on a cushion bench beneath the porthole, watching the tiny sparkles of dust that danced in the streak of light but dared not move.

They'd docked this morning before dawn in the caves by a beach and all day the men had been at work while she waited until evening for Wraith to call for her. Men had already begun making their way to level ground, where they'd secure horses and ride all the way to Dublin to see Viscount Loftford, the Lord Chancellor of Ireland.

A knock sounded swiftly, followed by one of the crewman ducking his head inside upon her call. "My lady, the cap'n awaits ye."

Faryn nodded and followed the crewman from

her cabin to the dinghy that was soon rowed to shore. She followed the wiry man through a break in the rock to a concealed pathway that led up the side of a cliff. The rock beneath her feet was slippery and she placed each foot very carefully, thankful for the new leather boots brought to her earlier in the day.

They reached the top of the cliff and she scanned the area, now completely covered in darkness. Even the moon seemed hidden.

"This way," the sailor whispered and tugged on her arm. They didn't walk long before coming upon Wraith and his small entourage, the clouds covering the moon moving in just enough time to gleam on her lover, almost as if revealing him there just for her.

He gave her a confident, knowing smile that sent shivers along her limbs and memories of the hours they'd spent alone swirling in her mind.

"We are in luck, *leannan*, for the Lord Chancellor is in Galway and not Dublin. Our trip will be less dangerous and only one night instead of four. And yet, still far enough away my ship and crew will be safe. Let us make haste."

She mounted the horse he indicated and they took off at a quick pace. He'd warned her it would be a rough journey with their speed, and having not ridden in several months, she wasn't exactly ready for the bone-jarring pace. Much more difficult was the fact that it was night and she could barely see in front of her, let alone the ground. They did not travel on the main road but through fields and forest. Consequently, she was in fear of being thrown the entire time.

Under the cover of darkness was the only way to travel, especially with a price on Wraith's head. Although Faryn doubted anyone would recognize him. Years had passed since he'd openly set foot in Ireland, and under his current guise he looked not so lordly, and quite the pirate.

Tight black breeches clung to long, muscled legs, which in turn clutched the horse he'd absconded with from a local stable. He'd forgone a jacket and wore only the black linen shirt he was partial to. At his hip was his plaid belt outfitted with weapons and on his hands black leather gloves. A black captain's hat sat atop his head, only slightly larger and more intimidating. His jaw was clenched tight, his eyes scanned the area. Faryn had trouble not staring when her gaze kept drifting—without her control— over his body. She watched the muscles ripple beneath the fabric of both his breeches and his linen shirt, the moonlight making him all the more mysterious and enticing. His thick arms, bunched and taut, as he wielded the reins of the horse. Without thinking, she licked her lips, imagining running her arms over the ridges and contours.

"My lady!" shouted Churl from her right.

She glanced ahead just in time to see what he

warned her of. Her horse headed straight for a foxhole in the ground. She tightened her grip on the reins and tugged left, within seconds clear of what could have been a disaster.

Her heart pounded in her ears and her breath had all but ceased. Wraith glanced at her with a frown but didn't stop his progress.

An accident was the last thing she needed, it would only solidify in his mind that he should not have brought her, and perhaps even push him to return her to her family. That could not happen under any circumstances until she'd had time to speak to Viscount Loftford herself—although she prayed she never saw her family again. Not after how they'd treated her, and what she'd recently learned of her father's involvement in the death of Wraith's family.

She kept her vision forward and did not chance to look at Wraith again, else she come within seconds of tragedy once more and destroy their mission for good.

By the time the sun made a pink line on the horizon the following morning, they'd reached the city of Galway. They easily entered and their horses were taken to the stables. Faryn waited on baited breath for Wraith to be immediately seized by guards, but they never came. Instead, the personal steward of the Lord Chancellor came forward and somehow, Wraith managed to obtain two adjoining rooms in the castle Viscount Loftford had claimed, as well as lodging for his men. He had said that the viscount had once been particularly fond of his father, but Faryn couldn't help but fear it was a trap.

A light knock sounded at her door. She moved away from the window she'd been gazing out of and opened the adjoining door to Wraith's room.

"Faryn," he said softly, and leaned down, pressing his lips to hers in a gentle caress. "Ye're not asleep yet?"

She shook her head. "I am too nervous."

"I am glad ye have yet to slumber, I've learned something."

"Come in," she said, tugging his hand.

He slipped into her room and drew her to the bed, where they lay down together, her head on his chest.

"Loftford will see me today, in secret. I had thought he would make me wait days, to agonize over our meeting, but he is preparing to see me after his morning mass and he breaks his fast."

She drew imaginary circles on his chest. "Wraith, that is wonderful." Then perhaps they could get back to the life they'd carved for themselves on the ship... if he would have her.

"There is more." But he didn't go on.

"What is it?" she asked, fearing what he would say.

"Your father and mother are also in residence."

She sat up, any bit of sleep that ebbed on the outskirts of her mind completely gone. "What?"

That trap she'd imagined felt like it had finally fallen down, caging her in.

"He seeks to beg the Lord Chancellor's favor in rewarding him with the earldom. I suppose he feels he deserves it since the king has not rewarded anyone with it. I understand your father works the lands now and provides knights to the king for it, yet the majority of the coin derived from it goes to the royal coffers."

"But they are your title and estates! Not his!"

"Aye." Wraith looked resigned to the fact.

Anger sliced through Faryn. How could her father, the man who'd sired her, be so evil? And what of her mother? Was she also so cruel, or did she have little to say, just watching from the dark corners as her husband wreaked havoc on mankind and got away with it? She had to remind herself that Wraith knew not what she did about her father's heinous crimes against his family. He only knew the man to be a bad father, not a murderer, too.

"I wish to come with ye when ye speak to Viscount Loftford." She came to her knees to kneel before him, her eyes beseeching.

"I dinna think 'tis a good idea." Wraith shook his head, his lips set in a firm line.

"Wraith," she implored, reaching out to grip his hands with hers. "I know ye dinna wish me to be in harm's way but if the king is as ye say, then I will be safe. At least then I willna be here where my father could find me if he gets word of our arrival. And…I couldna let ye go alone."

He smiled at her indulgently. "Ye're worried about me, *leannan*?"

"Aye." She hoped that he would allow her to go along with what she'd said. But if he still said no then she would find a way to go anyway.

"I suppose it canna hurt to have ye with me but ye must not interfere. Promise me."

"I wouldna dream of ruining your chances at freedom."

She said a silent prayer of thanks that it had been so easy to convince him to allow her to accompany him.

Wraith laid out the documents and evidence that he'd gathered over the years on a table in front of Loftford. The Lord Chancellor's eyes lit on the ring. Faryn saw the note of recognition that flared in his eyes.

She did as Wraith had asked and remained in the corner. She still wore the gown he'd given her before they'd disembarked from the ship but at least she'd had a chance to wash the grime of their ride from her person and her hair was neatly pulled up, curls falling around her cheeks. But for all her decorum, her insides were tied up in knots and she might have vomited if she'd eaten anything, and was glad she'd declined breaking her fast.

Wraith still looked the same as he always did to her—dangerous and delicious. But also calm and collected. He had a confidence about him that made others follow his lead.

Viscount Loftford had recognized him at once and his eyes had sparkled, even if his demeanor remained stoic. He sat poised in a high back chair on the dais.

"I have seen this ring before," Loftford said and his eyes locked on Wraith. "Havena ye?"

Wraith slowly shook his head. "It seems familiar to me but I dinna know whether 'tis from memory or from having stared at it so many times."

"'Tis a nobleman's ring. A man who is today at my court."

Wraith's gaze popped up from where he'd been gazing on the ring. "Here? Now?"

Loftford nodded.

Faryn opened her mouth to speak but nothing came out. She cleared her throat of the cobwebs caused by anxiety. "My lord," she managed to squeak.

"Come forward, child," he said.

She came forward curtsied.

"Did ye have something ye wished to say?"

She nodded, still looking at the ground. She swore she could feel the air in the room tighten along with Wraith's body. His anger was no doubt piqued at her now for interrupting.

"What is it?" Loftford's voice was gentle, as he must have had an idea of what she would say, since he knew from her introduction upon entering who she was. She'd seen the flash of recognition in his eyes along with the curiosity of her being with Wraith before he'd schooled his features.

"The ring… 'Tis my father's." There, she'd said it. Lightning had not struck her. She hadn't vomited. But beside her, an angry warmth raged from Wraith like fire. His hands were fisted at his sides and she couldn't meet his gaze.

"Aye, my lady," Loftford crooned. "Had ye any knowledge of his part in the crimes he committed against the Earl of Drohgard?"

"Nay." She shook her head vehemently. "I only knew when I saw the ring."

Loftford nodded, satisfied, but Wraith still stood beside her, deadly silent.

"There ye have it, lad, and I do believe ye. Baron Claneford will be arrested, his titles and lands forfeited. I shall have my men investigate the matter to see ye are cleared of the crimes."

Faryn's head nearly burst. So quick it was, and just like that, the Lord Chancellor had said he would arrest her father, he would look into clearing Wraith's name.

Her heart burst with pleasure and pride for

Wraith. He must be so relieved! All of his hard work, all his suffering was nearly to an end. And though she hated her father, she felt a sudden rush of fear for him. What would happen? Would they put him to death?

She caught Wraith's gaze and faltered. What she saw in front of her was the true Captain Wraith Noir. The one who did battle, the one who kidnapped innocents and murdered for riches. The dangerous pirate. His eyes were filled with rage when they met hers, and if looks could kill, she would be a pile of bones, muscle and flesh on the floor.

She'd known he would be upset with her, that he would see her as having lied to him, kept things from him, but she had not thought he would show her this level of outrage, this level of hatred.

"Ye lied to me. Ye deliberately kept the truth from me. Why do such a thing unless ye were a part of it? Unless ye sought from the very beginning to reel me into your family's web of treachery? Tell me, had your father heard that I'd be anchoring that night ye walked on the beach? Did he tell ye to spread your legs for me?"

Faryn blanched. Her stomach plummeted and her mouth went dry. Before Wraith could say another word to mortify her further, she fled from the room.

CHAPTER TWELVE

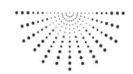

Faryn thought for sure her heart would burst within her chest. The pain seared through her with rising agony. She'd thought she'd prepared herself for his belief in her betrayal, even though it was furthest from the truth, but even that had not truly prepared her for how it felt to see the anger in his eyes.

Where once affection, desire and respect had filled his gaze, now it was replaced with something more sinister, a feeling she'd hoped to never experience but in the end had some inkling was coming. It felt as though he'd taken one of his blades and thrust it through her heart.

She ran blindly as tears filled her eyes and managed with awkward shaking hands to lift her skirts enough so that she didn't trip on their length.

"Oof!" With a thud, her flight halted against a

body and strong arms held her from falling onto the ground.

Through hazy eyes, she made out a figure— an all too familiar figure.

"Daughter!" Her father's growl cut through the racing thoughts in her mind.

She opened her mouth but no sound came out. She didn't know whether to scream or act as though she knew nothing, and her head swam and threatened to make her faint dead away.

"What are ye doing in Galway? Where have ye been? We have been looking for ye! Lord Bréagadóir has taken to the sea fearing ye were stolen by pirates."

He shook her like a rag doll, her head flopping back and forth, her teeth clicking together, when she did not speak to answer him.

"Do ye defy me? Have ye run away from your duty?" Spittle flew onto her face as he bellowed at her.

A crowd gathered around them, none too discreetly.

"How could ye?" The words slipped from her mouth before she could rein them in.

He narrowed his eyes at her, his grip on her arms tightening.

"Ye defy me and then dare to question me?"

She shook her head and bit her lip hard to keep from saying anything else.

"Answer me!" he bellowed again.

"Nay," she whispered. She tried not to look around as she sensed more people coming to watch their spectacle. Good God, she prayed Wraith did not see this!

Shouting from whence Lady Faryn had fled drew Wraith's and Loftford's attention.

"What is this?" the Lord Chancellor asked, irritation marring his features.

Wraith didn't wait to find out. For as much as he believed Faryn had betrayed him, he couldn't see her come to harm—at least by anyone other than himself.

He led the way from the viscount's receiving chamber through a series of doors until they came to a large crowd. In the center, a man held a woman by her arms as he bellowed in her face.

"Answer me!"

"Father, ye're a murderer! How could ye be so cruel, so evil?"

The baron's face blanched white, and even from this distance, Wraith watched Faryn's shoulders shake on her lithe frame.

Her father growled something under his breath and then yanked her with him, clearly intending to leave the area.

"Halt!" shouted the Lord Chancellor.

The baron continued to try to drag his daughter away but several of the nosy members of the court blocked his escape.

"The Lord Chancellor has ordered ye to stay where ye are," Wraith said, his voice deadly calm.

Slowly, Baron Claneford turned, recognition plain in his eyes as he viewed Wraith.

"Nay," he whispered, shaking his head as if he'd seen a ghost.

"Let the lady go," Wraith demanded. He avoided Faryn's gaze even though he could feel her eyes penetrating his soul.

"She is not just a lady but my daughter. She ran away from home and her marriage, and I must see that she is guarded. This is no concern of yours." Baron Claneford's meager attempt at playing nonchalant was not lost on Wraith.

"But it is my concern. She didna run but was taken. By me. She is mine."

If possible, Claneford's face paled even further.

"By ye? How?"

"Let her go. Ye and I have business of our own to attend to."

"Nay!" Claneford shouted. "Ye're dead! Your whole family is dead! I saw to it myself!"

"I assure ye, I am here in the flesh."

With Baron Claneford's last comment, Wraith saw from the corner of his eye Loftford wave to his men. Several guards surrounded the baron, who was forced to release his daughter.

He shoved her away and the force of the move

sent Faryn sprawling forward and knocked a couple of his guards off their steady feet. Wraith lunged to catch Faryn before she hit the floor but at the same time, the baron pulled a dagger from some part of his person. He waved his arm in an arc, the blade aimed at his daughter. Wraith changed his angle and nearly missed the downward plunge of Claneford's dagger. Faryn fell to the floor in a pile of skirts and wriggled away from the fray. Wraith clicked his ring, flicking his hand in time to leave a gash along the baron's arm.

The older man screeched in pain and dropped his dagger, reaching instead for his bleeding limb. The Lord Chancellor's men took the opportunity to grab Claneford and drag him away.

Wraith stood and held out his hand to Faryn. She stared up at him, confusion in her eyes.

"Forgive me?" he asked.

She nodded silently and took his hand.

"Ye're not your father. I know ye. I know ye for the innocent and kind-hearted woman ye are. I spoke out of anger." He pulled her into an embrace, not caring that they had an audience. She sagged against him and the gentle shaking of her shoulders told him she was crying. He had never wanted to hurt her, nor see tears in her eyes, and yet here she was sobbing quietly against his shoulder. He leaned down, kissed her atop her head, and then whispered in her ear.

"Hush now, *leannan*. Dinna cry. All will be well. We shall be together just as we dreamed of."

She looked up at him, her eyes watery, her lips red where she'd bitten them. He bent down and pressed his lips to hers, savoring her taste and her affection.

Against her lips he whispered, "I love ye, Faryn."

Her voice cracked on a sob with her reply. "I love ye, too."

"'Lo there." The Lord Chancellor's voice cut through their reverie. "Ian, cease manhandling the maiden."

"Ian?" Faryn asked, pulling away to glance at him quizzically.

Wraith shrugged, a wicked grin curving his lips. He realized they'd never gotten around to him telling her his true name. "'Tis not so dreadful and mysterious as Wraith."

She chuckled at this. "Nay, but suits ye all the same."

"My lord," he said, turning to face the Lord Chancellor, their hands gripped tightly together. "Might I have your permission to marry this fair maiden?"

Viscount Loftford's eyes sparkled. "Ye may inquire, Lord Drohgard, and I am happy to give ye my blessing."

"Lord Drohgard…" Wraith's voice trailed off.

"Aye, ye have proven your innocence, and I have

waited these past years for ye to return to your rightful place. However, there is one condition of my gift."

Wraith stiffened, lowered his eyes. What could the Lord Chancellor ask? "Aye, my lord."

Loftford lifted his chin in challenge. "Ye have pirated our shores and taken the innocent. If ye wish to fully receive a pardon, your title, your lands, ye must first retrieve the Irish men and women ye adducted."

The Lord Chancellor's demand would be a daunting task. But it was one Wraith was eager to complete, and with Faryn by his side. Orelia kept good records of her human booty, and once he had a hold of where each one was finally taken, he could easily begin retrieving them—which he would relish as he'd never wanted to be a party to such a thing, but his safety had required he be the deliveryman. With the help of his brethren, the Devils of the Deep would see that every man, woman and child were accounted for. 'Twas also a chance to seek vengeance on the pirate queen who'd tormented him.

"My lord, as ye wish." He bowed before the king and when he rose addressed him once more. "A boon?"

Loftford nodded.

"Might I marry first, so my lady can accompany me on the seas?"

The viscount grinned knowingly. "Och, aye, as soon as possible."

Wraith too broke out into a grin. Excitement coursed through his veins, for together he and Faryn would travel the world re-abducting those he'd enslaved to others and pirating pirates who would seek their fortunes on the high seas.

EPILOGUE

Six Months Later

Wraith wrapped one strong arm beneath Faryn's knees and another behind her back and lifted her into the air. He carried her through the door of their cabin aboard *The Avenger* and toward the bed, where he gently laid her down before covering her with his body.

"We did it, my love," he whispered, nipping at her lips with his teeth.

Faryn wrapped her arms around him and pulled him closer for a kiss. Their mouths connected in an arousing melding of tongue and lips.

"And now we shall sail back to Ireland?" she asked, panting from how his kisses always seemed to take her breath away, make her blood pump hard through her veins and send her body singing.

"Perhaps."

"Perhaps not?"

He chuckled and buried his face in the crook of her neck. Faryn arched her back and tilted her head to the side, allowing him a greater expanse of her flesh to kiss and suck.

"'Tis true we have recaptured the innocent. Thank ye Gods Queen Orelia sold all of them to only a select few. But I thought for us to drop them on an Irish beach before sailing to a remote island, where I might enjoy your body for days on end, until we can both no longer stand, without taking on any further responsibilities."

His hands traveled over her ribs, down her hips and to her thighs, where he gripped her behind the knees and pulled them up around his waist so he might settle between her legs. His rigid cock pressed against her heat, which was already wet with wanting.

He rocked back and forth against her, sending frissons of desire and need sparkling through her limbs.

"Mmm…aye…" she moaned, arching her back and undulating her hips in time with his.

"Not so fast, *leannan*. I want to make love to ye all night."

He stood abruptly and pulled her up with him. The light faded through the porthole, bathing them in an ethereal tranquility. The ship swayed back and forth against the dock. Save for a few men on watch, the rest of the crew and the brethren were in port, no doubt at a tavern or whorehouse, as the captain had given them the night off as thanks for all their hard work.

"I love ye with a fierceness that grips me right here." He tapped his chest.

Faryn reached up and pressed a palm to his chest, then trailed her hand lower to pull the linen shirt from his breeches. She trailed her hand beneath the fabric up his smooth stomach to his chest and again flattened her hand over his heart. She could feel the strong, steady beat of that organ beneath her fingertips. Wraith—for she had a hard time thinking of him as Ian—placed his hand over hers and threaded his other hand through her hair.

Their gazes locked in an intense stare—gray passionate storm clouds melded with blue desire.

"I love ye, too," she whispered. "I could never live without ye."

Wraith growled from deep in his chest and hauled her against him, his mouth coming down on hers with a fierce craving, claiming her once again. The stark, raw passion in their kiss was unmatched by any other kiss. They had been through so much together, learned so much from each other, and still come out on top, thriving, loving. Their lips slanted back and forth, teeth nipping, tongues sucking.

Hungrily they tore at their clothes, wanting

nothing more than to press heated flesh to heated flesh. When finally neither wore a stitch of cloth, they pressed their bodies together, gasping at the silky sensation of her soft warm flesh against his sinewy hot length.

Her hands rubbed up and down his body, massaging the muscles of his back, buttocks and flanks, over his taut arms, broad shoulders and the ridges of his chest and stomach. Fingers swirled around his nipples and gently toyed with the crisp yet soft chest hair. She paused just short of his hard, thick cock to run her hands back over the muscles of his strong form.

He let his hands trail over her rounded hips, tight buttocks, lithe thighs, flat belly and supple breasts. She'd taken to using a sugaring technique Orelia had shown her, and now every inch of her body was smooth and hairless. Unable to wait a moment longer, he trailed his fingers in a path to her core, where he grazed between the bare folds of her sex, where she was slick with moisture. He delved two fingers inside her, groaning when she moaned and arched against him, her channel tightening.

With slow, torturous movements, he pulled his fingers out only to push them back inside, his mouth making a path from her lips to her neck and to her breasts.

"Your skin tastes heavenly to a man as full of sin

as myself." He drew a nipple into his mouth and sucked hard.

She shuddered and threaded her fingers through his hair.

"The day ye found me upon the beach was a day that forever changed our lives. If it is sin, then I will gladly sin with ye."

She lifted a leg and hooked it behind his thigh, pressing her hips forward so she might feel the length of him against her more fully.

"Oh God, Faryn," he murmured against her flesh. "I want this to last forever but I am swiftly losing control."

"Then lose it. Take us both to ecstasy," she breathed in his ear and nipped his lobe. She reached between them and gripped his arousal. She stroked up and down his shaft, teasing the head with her thumb. Gliding it over her core and pressing the tip to the center.

"I think I will," he promised.

Wraith lifted Faryn's other leg to hook around his waist, so she was wrapped around him. He carried her to the bed, where he sat down, Faryn still straddling his lap. She rolled her hips against him, pressed her breasts to his chest and captured his lips in hers. He teased her mouth with his teeth and tongue. His hands gripped her buttocks, massaging, stroking.

"I want to be inside ye," he whispered against

her mouth.

"Aye, please," she whimpered.

Wraith gripped her hips and lifted her up, positioning his himself at her entrance. He slipped the tip in just a bit and held her still. The muscles of her sheath clenched tight and she tried to press down, to take him in farther, but he wouldn't let her.

"Not yet," he murmured.

He pulled out, rubbing his length between her folds, over her pearl, back and forth, the same way she had teased him. Her moans deepened and she rocked against him. Her whole body hummed with need and desire. He slipped the tip inside her again, teasing them both. She gyrated her hips and begged for him to plunge deep but still he made her wait.

Her stomach clenched, her nipples were hard and tight, her pleasure bud throbbed and she wanted nothing more than for him to take her to ecstasy and back.

She reached her hand between them, gripped him and stroked up and down with fervor. He was so hard in her hand, slick from her essence, and she could feel the pulse of his blood as it pumped harder.

She positioned him at her opening and locked her gaze with his. "Take me, Wraith."

He gripped her hips tight and thrust upward, impaling her.

Her head fell back and her body stretched to fit

him. Her entire length tingled and inside she pulsed with delicious need.

Wraith pressed his lips to her breasts and lifted her only to pull her back down, burying himself deep within her. They moved together rhythmically. Her lifting her hips and him thrusting back inside but doing it with torturous slowness. Neither one wanting to climax right away, both wanting to let the pleasure build up with a power neither one could comprehend.

Their limbs shook, sweat trickled down their spines and still they moved at that slow, sensual pace. Faryn curled her arms around Wraith's neck and he leaned up to capture her lips in an erotic swirl of tongue and lips, tasting, licking, nipping.

Lost in their kiss, they moved their bodies faster. In and out, up and down. Hips pressing forward and back. Tongue caressing tongue. Breaths were hitched. Hearts beat a rapid pace as one.

Then a slow rumbling started from the core of Faryn's being—a vibration from the inside out. And, as if the ship had fired its cannons, they both exploded into mind-numbing, body-shattering climax. Their bodies shook with pleasure, until finally they collapsed against each other onto the bed in a sweaty, tingling heap of limbs.

Lazy hands stroked up and down sated bodies as they caught their breath.

"'Tis a wonder to me that every young lady does

not wish to be a pirate's bounty," Faryn murmured on a sigh.

Wraith's chest rumbled against her ear as he chuckled. "Ye, *leannan*, were a booty well worth taking."

If you enjoyed A PIRATE'S BOUNTY, please spread the word by leaving a review on the site where you purchased your copy, or a reader site such as Goodreads or Shelfari! I love to hear from readers too, so drop me a line at authorelizaknight@gmail.com *OR visit me on Facebook:* https://www.facebook.com/elizaknightfiction. I'm also on Twitter: @ElizaKnight. If you'd like to receive my occasional newsletter, please sign up at www.elizaknight.com. *Many thanks!*

ABOUT THE AUTHOR

Eliza Knight is an award-winning and *USA Today* bestselling indie author of over fifty sizzling historical romance and erotic romance. Under the name E. Knight, she pens rip-your-heart-out historical fiction. While not reading, writing or researching for her latest book, she chases after her three children. In her spare time (if there is such a thing…) she likes daydreaming, wine-tasting, traveling, hiking, staring at the stars, watching movies, shopping and visiting with family and friends. She lives atop a small mountain with her own knight in shining armor, three princesses and two very naughty puppies. Visit Eliza at http://www.elizaknight.com or her historical blog History Undressed: www.historyundressed.com. Sign up for her newsletter to get news about books, events, contests and sneak peaks! http://eepurl.com/CSFFD

- facebook.com/elizaknightfiction
- twitter.com/elizaknight
- instagram.com/elizaknightfiction
- bookbub.com/authors/eliza-knight
- goodreads.com/elizaknight
- pinterest.com/authoreknight

ALSO BY ELIZA KNIGHT

PIRATES OF BRITANNIA: DEVILS OF THE DEEP

Savage of the Sea
The Sea Devil
A Pirate's Bounty

THE STOLEN BRIDE SERIES

The Highlander's Temptation
The Highlander's Reward
The Highlander's Conquest
The Highlander's Lady
The Highlander's Warrior Bride
The Highlander's Triumph
The Highlander's Sin
Wild Highland Mistletoe (a Stolen Bride winter novella)
The Highlander's Charm (a Stolen Bride novella)
A Kilted Christmas Wish – a contemporary Holiday spin-off

The Highlander's Gift

THE CONQUERED BRIDE SERIES

Conquered by the Highlander
Seduced by the Laird
Taken by the Highlander (a Conquered bride novella)
Claimed by the Warrior
Stolen by the Laird
Protected by the Laird (a Conquered bride novella)
Guarded by the Warrior

THE MACDOUGALL LEGACY SERIES

Laird of Shadows
Laird of Twilight
Laird of Darkness

THE THISTLES AND ROSES SERIES

Promise of a Knight
Eternally Bound
Breath from the Sea

THE HIGHLAND BOUND SERIES (EROTIC TIME-TRAVEL)

Behind the Plaid
Bared to the Laird
Dark Side of the Laird
Highlander's Touch
Highlander Undone
Highlander Unraveled

WICKED WOMEN

Her Desperate Gamble
Seducing the Sheriff
Kiss Me, Cowboy

∽

UNDER THE NAME E. KNIGHT

TALES FROM THE TUDOR COURT

My Lady Viper

Prisoner of the Queen

ANCIENT HISTORICAL FICTION

A Day of Fire: a novel of Pompeii
A Year of Ravens: a novel of Boudica's Rebellion

EXCERPT FROM THE HIGHLANDER'S GIFT

CHAPTER ONE

Dupplin Castle
Scottish Highlands
Winter, 1318

Sir Niall Oliphant had lost something.

Not a trinket, or a boot. Not a pair of hose, or even his favorite mug. Nothing as trivial as that. In fact, he wished it *was* so minuscule that he could simply replace it. What'd he'd lost was devastating, and yet it felt entirely selfish given some of those closest to him had lost their lives.

He was still here, living and breathing. He was still walking around on his own two feet. Still handsome in the face. Still able to speak coherently, even if he didn't want to.

But he couldn't replace what he'd lost.

What he'd lost would irrevocably change his life, his entire future. It made him want to back into the darkest corner and let his life slip away, to forget about even having a future at all. To give everything he owned to his brother and say goodbye. He was useless now. Unworthy.

Niall cleared the cobwebs that had settled in his throat by slinging back another dram of whisky. The shutters in his darkened bedchamber were closed tight, the fire long ago grown cold. He didn't allow candles in the room, nor visitors. So when a knock sounded at his door, he ignored it, preferring to chug his spirits from the bottle rather than pouring it into a cup.

The knocking grew louder, more insistent.

"Go away," he bellowed, slamming the whisky down on the side table beside where he sat, and hearing the clay jug shatter. A shard slid into his finger, stinging as the liquor splashed over it. But he didn't care.

This pain, pain in his only index finger, he wanted to have. Wanted a reminder there was still some part of him left. Part of him that could still feel and bleed. He tried to ignore that part of him that wanted to be alive, however small it was.

The handle on the door rattled, but Niall had

barred it the day before. Refusing anything but whisky. Maybe he could drink himself into an oblivion he'd never wake from. Then all of his worries would be gone forever.

"Niall, open the bloody door."

The sound of his brother's voice through the cracks had Niall's gaze widening slightly. Walter was a year younger than he was. And still whole. Walter had tried to understand Niall's struggle, but what man could who'd not been through it himself?

"I said go away, ye bloody whoreson." His words slurred, and he went to tipple more of the liquor only to recall he'd just shattered it everywhere.

Hell and damnation. The only way to get another bottle would be to open the door.

"I'll pretend I didna hear ye just call our dear mother a whore. Open the damned door, or I'll take an axe to it."

Like hell he would. Walter was the least aggressive one in their family. Sweet as a lad, he'd grown into a strong warrior, but he was also known as the heart of the Oliphant clan. The idea of him chopping down a door was actually funny. Outside, the corridor grew silent, and Niall leaned his head back against the chair, wondering how long he had until his brother returned, and if it was enough time to sneak down to the cellar and get another jug of whisky.

Needless to say, when a steady thwacking

sounded at the door—reminding Niall quite a bit like the heavy side of an axe—he sat up straighter and watched in drunken fascination as the door started to splinter. Shards of wood came flying through the air as the hole grew larger and the sound of the axe beating against the surface intensified.

Walter had grown some bloody ballocks.

Incredible.

Didn't matter. What would Walter accomplish by breaking down the door? What could he hope would happen?

Niall wasn't going to leave the room or accept food.

Niall wasn't going to move on with his life.

So he sat back and waited, curious more than anything as to what Walter's plan would be once he'd gained entry.

Just as tall and broad of shoulder as Niall, Walter kicked through the remainder of the door and ducked through the ragged hole.

"That's enough." Walter looked down at Niall, his face fierce, reminding him very much of their father when they were lads.

"That's enough?" Niall asked, trying to keep his eyes wide but having a hard time. The light from the corridor gave his brother a darkened, shadowy look.

"Ye've sat in this bloody hell hole for the past three days." Walter gestured around the room. "Ye stink of shite. Like a bloody pig has laid waste to your chamber."

"Are ye calling me a shite pig?" Niall thought about standing up, calling his brother out, but that seemed like too much effort.

"Mayhap I am. Will it make ye stand up any faster?"

Niall pursed his lips, giving the impression of actually considering it. "Nay."

"That's what I thought. But I dinna care. Get up."

Niall shook his head slowly. "I'd rather not."

"I'm not asking."

My, my. Walter's ballocks were easily ten times than Niall had expected. The man was bloody testing him to be sure.

"Last time I checked, I was the eldest," Niall said.

"Ye might have been born first, but ye lost your mind some time ago, which makes me the better fit for making decisions."

Niall hiccupped. "And what decisions would ye be making, wee brother?"

"Getting your arse up. Getting ye cleaned up. Airing out the gongheap."

"Doesna smell so bad in here." Niall gave an exaggerated sniff, refusing to admit that Walter was indeed correct. It smelled horrendous.

"I'm gagging, brother. I might die if I have to stay much longer."

"Then by all means, pull up a chair."

"Ye're an arse."

"No more so than ye."

"Not true."

Niall sighed heavily. "What do ye want? Why would ye make me leave? I've nothing to live for anymore."

"Ye've eight-thousand reasons to live, ye blind goat."

"Eight thousand?"

"A random number." Walter waved his hand and kicked at something on the floor. "Ye've the people of your clan, the warriors ye lead, your family. The woman ye're betrothed to marry. Everyone is counting on ye, and ye must come out of here and attend to your duties. Ye've mourned long enough."

"How can ye presume to tell me that I've mourned long enough? Ye know nothing." A slow boiling rage started in Niall's chest. All these men telling him how to feel. All these men thinking they knew better. A bunch of bloody ballocks!

"Aye, I've not lost what ye have, brother. Ye're right. I dinna know what 'tis like to be ye, either. But I know what 'tis like to be the one down in the hall waiting for ye to come and take care of your business. I know what 'tis like to look upon the faces of the clan as they worry about whether they'll be raided or ravaged while their leader sulks in a vat of whisky and does nothing to care for them."

Niall gritted his teeth. No one understood. And he didn't need the reminder of his constant failings.

"Then take care of it," Niall growled, jerking forward fast enough that his vision doubled. "Ye've always wanted to be first. Ye've always wanted what was mine. Go and have it. Have it all."

Walter took a step back as though Niall had hit him. "How can ye say that?" Even in the dim light, Niall could see the pain etched on his brother's features. Aye, what he'd said was a lie, but it had made him feel better all the same.

"Ye heard me. Get the fuck out." Niall moved to push himself from the chair, remembered too late how difficult that would be, and fell back into it. Instead, he let out a string of curses that had Walter shaking his head.

"Ye need to get yourself together, decide whether or not ye are going to turn your back on this clan. Do it for yourself. Dinna go down like this. Ye are still Sir Niall fucking Oliphant. Warrior. Heir to the chiefdom of Oliphant. Hero. Leader. Brother. Soon to be husband and father."

Walter held his gaze unwaveringly. A torrent of emotion jabbed from that dark look into Niall's chest, crushing his heart.

"Get out," he said again through gritted teeth, feeling the pain of rejecting his brother acutely.

They'd always been so close. And even though he

was pushing him away, he also desperately wanted to pull him closer.

He wanted to hug him tightly, to tell him not to worry, that soon enough he'd come out of the dark and be the man Walter once knew. But those were all lies, for he would never be the same again, and he couldn't see how he would ever be able to exit this room and attempt a normal life.

"Ye're not the only one who's lost a part of himself," Walter muttered as he ducked beneath the door. "I want my brother back."

"Your brother is dead."

At that, Walter paused. He turned back around, a snarl poised on his lips, and Niall waited longingly for whatever insult would come out. Any chance to engage in a fight, but then Walter's face softened. "Maybe he is."

With those soft words uttered, he disappeared, leaving behind the gaping hole and the shattered wood on the floor, a haunting mirror image to the wide-open wound Niall felt in his soul.

Niall glanced down to his left, at the sleeve that hung empty at his side, a taunting reminder of his failure in battle. Warrior. Ballocks! Not even close.

When he considered lying down on the ground and licking the whisky from the floor, he knew it was probably time to leave his chamber. But he was no good to anyone outside of his room. Perhaps he could prove that fact once and for all, then Walter would leave him be. And he knew his brother spoke the truth about smelling like a pig. He'd not bathed in days. If he was going to prove he was worthless as a leader now, he would do so smelling decent, so people took him seriously rather than believing him to be mad.

Slipping through the hole in the door, he walked noiselessly down the corridor to the stairs at the rear used by the servants, tripping only once along the way. He attempted to steal down the winding steps, a feat that nearly had him breaking his neck. In fact, he took the last dozen steps on his arse. Once he reached the entrance to the side of the bailey, he lifted the bar and shoved the door open, the cool wind a welcome blast against his heated skin. With the sun set, no one saw him creep outside and slink along the stone as he made his way to the stables and the massive water trough kept for the horses. He might as well bathe there, like the animal he was.

Trough in sight, he staggered forward and tumbled headfirst into the icy water.

Niall woke sometime later, still in the water, but turned over at least. He didn't know whether to be grateful he'd not drowned. His clothes were soaked, and his legs hung out on either side of the wooden trough. It was still dark, so at least he'd not slept through the night in the chilled water.

He leaned his head back, body covered in wrinkled gooseflesh and teeth chattering, and stared up at the sky. Stars dotted the inky-black landscape and swaths of clouds streaked across the moon, as if one of the gods had swiped his hand through it, trying to wipe it away. But the moon was steadfast. Silver and bright and ever present. Returning as it should each night, though hiding its beauty day after day until it was just a sliver that made one wonder if it would return.

What was he doing out here? Not just in the tub freezing his idiot arse off, but here in this world? Why hadn't he been taken? Why had only part of him been stolen? Cut away…

Niall shuddered, more from the memory of that moment when his enemy's sword had cut through his armor, skin, muscle and bone. The crunching sound. The incredible pain.

He squeezed his eyes shut, forcing the memories away.

This is how he'd been for the better part of four months. Stumbling drunk and angry about the castle when he wasn't holed up in his chamber. Yelling at his brother, glowering at his father and mother, snapping at anyone who happened to cross his path. He'd become everything he hated.

There had been times he'd thought about ending it all. He always came back to the simple question that was with him now as he stared up at the large face of the moon.

"Why am I still here?" he murmured.

"Likely because ye havena pulled your arse out of the bloody trough."

Walter.

Niall's gaze slid to the side to see his brother standing there, arms crossed over his chest. "Are ye my bloody shadow? Come to tell me all my sins?"

"When will ye see I'm not the enemy? I want to help."

Niall stared back up at the moon, silently asking what he should do, begging for a sign.

Walter tugged at his arm. "Come on. Get out of the trough. Ye're not a pig as much as ye've been acting the part. Let us get ye some food."

Niall looked over at his little brother, perhaps seeing him for the first time. His throat felt tight, closing in on itself as a well of emotion overflowed from somewhere deep in his gut.

"Why do ye keep trying to help me? All I've done is berate ye for it."

"Aye. That's true, but I know ye speak from pain. Not from your heart."

"I dinna think I have a heart left."

Walter rolled his eyes and gave a swift tug, pulling him halfway from the trough. Though Niall was weak from lack of food and too much whisky, he managed to get himself the rest of the way out. He stood in the moonlight, dripping water around the near frozen ground.

"Ye have a heart. Ye have a soul. One arm. That is all ye've lost. Ye still have your manhood, aye?"

Niall shrugged. Aye, he still had his bloody cock, but what woman wanted a decrepit man heaving overtop of her with his mangled body in full view.

"I know what ye're thinking," Walter said. "And the answer is, every eligible maiden and all her friends. Not to mention the kitchen wenches, the widows in the glen, and their sisters."

"Ballocks," Niall muttered.

"Ye're still handsome. Ye're still heir to a powerful clan. Wake up, man. This is not ye. Ye canna let the loss of your arm be the destruction of your whole life. Ye're not the first man to ever be maimed in battle. Dinna be a martyr."

"Says the man with two arms."

"Ye want me to cut it off? I'll bloody do it." Walter turned in a frantic circle as if looking for the closest thing with a sharp edge.

Niall narrowed his eyes, silent, watching, waiting. When had his wee brother become such an intense force? Walter marched toward the barn, hand on the door, yanked it wide as if to continue the blockhead search. Niall couldn't help following after his brother who marched forward with purpose, disappearing inside the barn.

A flutter of worry dinged in Niall's stomach. Walter wouldn't truly go through with something so stupid, would he?

When he didn't immediately reappear, Niall's pang of worry heightened into dread. Dammit, he just might. With all the changes Walter had made recently, there was every possibility that he'd gone mad. Well, Niall might wish to disappear, but not before he made certain his brother was all right.

With a groan, Niall lurched forward, grabbed the door and yanked it open. The stables were dark and smelled of horses, leather and hay. He could hear a few horses nickering, and the soft snores of the stable hands up on the loft fast asleep.

"Walter," he hissed. "Enough. No more games."

Still, there was silence.

He stepped farther into the barn, and the door closed behind him, blocking out all the light save for a few strips that sank between cracks in the roof.

His feet shuffled silently on the dirt floor. Where the bloody hell had his brother gone?

And why was his heart pounding so fiercely? He trudged toward the first set of stables, touching the wood of the gates. A horse nudged his hand with its soft muzzle, blowing out a soft breath that tickled his palm, and Niall's heart squeezed.

"Prince," he whispered, leaning his forehead down until he felt it connect with the warm, solidness of his warhorse. Prince nickered and blew out another breath.

Niall had not ridden in months. If not for his horse, he might be dead. But rather than be irritated

Prince had done his job, he felt nothing but pride that the horse he'd trained from a colt into a mammoth had done his duty.

After Niall's arm had been severed and he was left for dead, Prince had nudged him awake, bent low and nipped at Niall's legs until he'd managed to crawl and heave himself belly first over the saddle. Prince had taken him home like that, a bleeding sack of grain.

Having thought him dead, the clan had been shocked and surprised to see him return, and that's when the true battle for his life had begun. He'd lost so much blood, succumbed to fever, and stopped breathing more than once. Hell, it was a miracle he was still alive.

Which begged the question—*why, why, why...*

"He's missed ye." Walter was beside him, and Niall jerked toward his brother, seeing his outline in the dark.

"Is that why ye brought me in here?"

"Did ye really think I'd cut off my arm?" Walter chuckled. "Ye know I like to fondle a wench and drink at the same time."

Niall snickered. "Ye're an arse."

"Aye, 'haps I am."

They were silent for a few minutes, Niall deep in thought as he stroked Prince's soft muzzle. His mind was a torment of unanswered questions. "Walter, I... I dinna know what to do."

"Take it one day at a time, brother. But do take it. No more being locked in your chamber."

Niall nodded even though his brother couldn't see him. A phantom twinge of pain rippled through the arm that was no longer there, and he stopped himself from moving to rub the spot, not wanting to humiliate himself in front of his brother. When would those pains go away? When would his body realize his arm had long since become bone in the earth?

One day at a time. That was something he might be able to do. "I'll have bad days."

"Aye. And good ones, too."

Niall nodded. He longed to saddle Prince and go for a ride but realized he wasn't even certain how to mount with only one arm to grab hold of the saddle. "I have so much to learn."

"Aye. But as I recall, ye're a fast learner."

"I'll start training again tomorrow."

"Good."

"But I willna be laird. Walter, the right to rule is yours now."

"Ye've time before ye need to make that choice. Da is yet breathing and making a ruckus."

"Aye. But I want ye to know what's coming. No matter what, I canna do that. I have to learn to pull on my bloody shirt first."

Walter slapped him on the back and squeezed his shoulder. "The lairdship is yours, with or without a shirt. Only thing I want is my brother back."

Niall drew in a long, mournful breath. "I'm not sure he's coming back. Ye'll have to learn to deal with me, the new me."

"New ye, old ye, still *ye*."

Want to read the rest of The Highlander's Gift?